"You're a confusing woman, Jenny Murdock."

"How's that?" she asked.

"You seem so close to your family. I can't figure out why you decided to come all the way to Wyoming."

To be me, she wanted to shout. "I'll have to introduce you to my brothers. They've been trying to run my life for the past twenty-six years. But I finally managed to get even."

"By coming here," Luke said. "And how do they feel about you going off and looking for a husband?" He teased.

"I told you, I'm not looking for anything."

"Well, sweetheart, nearly everyone in town is looking at you. There wasn't a man in the diner who didn't turn his head when you walked in." Luke knew it was only a matter of time before someone snatched her up. His only fear was it wouldn't be him....

Dear Reader,

What a month of wonderful reading Romance has for you! Our FABULOUS FATHERS title, *Most Wanted Dad,* continues Arlene James's miniseries THIS SIDE OF HEAVEN. Single dad and police officer Evans Kincaid can't quite handle his daughter's wild makeup and hairdos. Luckily—or not so luckily—the pretty lady next door is full of advice....

Do You Take This Child? is the last book of Marie Ferrarella's THE BABY OF THE MONTH CLUB miniseries—and our BUNDLES OF JOY title. Any-minute-mom-to-be Dr. Sheila Pollack expects to raise her baby all alone. But when the *long-absent* dad-to-be suddenly bursts into the delivery room, Sheila says "I do" between huffs and puffs!

In *Reilly's Bride* by Patricia Thayer, Jenny Murdock moves to Last Hope, Wyoming, to escape becoming a bride. But the town's crawling with eligible bachelors who want wives. So why isn't she happy when she falls for the one man who doesn't want to walk down the aisle?

Carla Cassidy continues THE BAKER BROOD miniseries with *Mom in the Making.* Single dad Russ Blackburn's little son chases away every woman who comes near his dad. It just figures the boy would like Bonnie Baker—a woman without a shred of mother material in her!

And don't miss the handsome drifter who becomes a woman's birthday present in Lauryn Chandler's *Her Very Own Husband,* or the two adorable kids who want their parents together in Robin Nicholas's *Wrangler's Wedding.*

Enjoy!

Melissa Senate,
Senior Editor

Please address questions and book requests to:
Silhouette Reader Service
U.S.: 3010 Walden Ave., P.O. Box 1325, Buffalo, NY 14269
Canadian: P.O. Box 609, Fort Erie, Ont. L2A 5X3

REILLY'S
BRIDE

Patricia Thayer

Silhouette
R O M A N C E™
Published by Silhouette Books
America's Publisher of Contemporary Romance

Dedication

My sisters, Lynn, Mary, Nancy and Julie.
From the dreams and secrets we've shared,
through the pain and the tears, we survived. I love you all.

Acknowledgment

To my friends Judy and Leo Carr, thanks for going out of your way to help me. And to Terry and Mary Spade, who showed me the beauty of Wyoming. I couldn't have done it without you.

 SILHOUETTE BOOKS

ISBN 0-373-19146-4

REILLY'S BRIDE

Copyright © 1996 by Patricia Wright

Printed in U.S.A.

Books by Patricia Thayer

Silhouette Romance

Just Maggie #895
Race to the Altar #1009
The Cowboy's Courtship #1064
Wildcat Wedding #1086
Reilly's Bride #1146

PATRICIA THAYER

was born and raised in Indiana and now resides in Southern California. Happily married for over twenty years and having three sons, she adores the attention she gets being the only female in the house. Besides writing, she enjoys doing research almost as much, especially when it means she has to travel! Pat also loves long walks, hand-holding and quiet talks with her best friend, her husband, Steve.

Her first book, *Just Maggie*, released in '92, received second place in the *Reader's Choice Awards*.

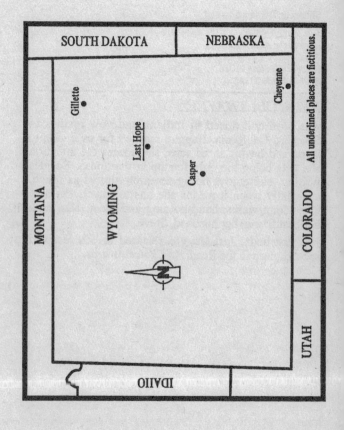

SOUTH DAKOTA

NEBRASKA

All underlined places are fictitious.

Cheyenne

Gillette

Last Hope

Casper

MONTANA

WYOMING

N

COLORADO

UTAH

IDAHO

Prologue

"I want you two to stop interfering in my life." Jennifer Murdock faced down her mother and two brothers, Tyler and Brett, in the office at the Murdock Ranch. She knew she was interrupting business, but she didn't care.

Brett raised his head. "Hi, Jen." Tyler ignored her.

"Don't give me that innocent act. I know what you guys have been up to."

That got Caroline Murdock's attention. "What happened?"

Jenny walked farther into the room. "I just got off the phone with Jeff Keller." Her hands were shaking. "I broke our date for tonight."

Tyler, the eldest, stood. At six foot two he looked intimidating with his deep-set dark eyes and chiseled features. But Jenny, nearly twelve years younger, had always known how to work him to get just what she wanted. Until now. She hadn't been able to get through to either of her brothers that she didn't need them hovering over her anymore.

Her mother came around the desk. "Honey, are you

feeling all right?''

"I feel lousy." Jenny looked at Brett who seemed very interested in a groove in the old desk top. It didn't matter, though, she had already had it out with him the day before at the office. Now, she needed to get a few things straight with Tyler. "I just want to know how far you were planning to go with this scheme."

Tyler's silence was as good as an admission of guilt.

"Or were you just going to let me marry a man who was more interested in securing an executive position at Murdock Oil than he was in me? How dare you try and buy me a husband!" Jenny's entire body trembled as she glanced at the shocked look on her mother's face. Thank God! Caroline wasn't in on it.

Tyler squared his shoulders. "Look, most guys you've brought around here aren't fit to—''

"Aren't fit to what? Marry a Murdock?" Jenny finished, then laughed. "That's funny. Most men I want to date won't have anything to do with me because of the two of you. You've threatened every man that comes within fifty feet of me. I should have guessed when Jeff approached me in the office that something was up."

Brett remained silent as Tyler spoke, "I wouldn't get involved in your life if you had the sense to stay away from losers. Remember last year when you got tangled up with that Thompson character? The man spent nearly every night getting juiced up at the Long Horn Saloon." Tyler shot her a glare that reminded her too much of her father. "That isn't the type of guy I want my sister dating. I'd prefer—''

"You'd prefer!" she repeated, her temper reaching the boiling point. "Who made you my keeper?"

"Hey, I've been getting you out of scrapes since you were a kid," he reminded her.

"Have you looked at me lately, Ty?" she asked. "I'm all grown-up. I don't need you to take care of me anymore."

Tyler tossed her a frustrated look. "How can I stand by and watch you get your heart broken by scum like Randy?"

"So you decided to find someone suitable like Jefferson Keller." She felt tears building behind her eyes. "Tell me, Ty, was it hard to find a man to go out with me? What did it cost you? Was there a seduction included in the deal? A marriage proposal?"

"Stop it!" he ordered. "It wasn't like that, Jen."

"Oh no? Surely Jeff was going to get something in return." Jenny had never felt so humiliated.

Tyler and Brett exchanged a glance but neither denied anything. "Jen, believe me," Tyler said, "Jeff was the one who showed an interest in you."

Caroline turned to her son. "I'm sure there are more details to this story, but so far I don't like what I'm hearing."

Jenny got a little satisfaction seeing the embarrassed looks on her brothers' faces. But she knew this wasn't going to be the last of their interference. Tyler would keep doing what he'd been doing since she was a little girl, trying to protect her from all the bad things in the world. Though she loved him with all her heart, it was past time she broke the ties. Tyler had Maggie and the kids. Brett had his new wife, Jessie. And Jenny wanted a life of her own. But, it still didn't make her decision any easier.

"I'm a big girl now. I graduated college...finally." That brought a smile from Brett and a sneer from Tyler. "And I'm going to apply for a job."

Brett's smile faded. "But you're already working, for Murdock Oil."

"In a job that you made up for me."

"When you get some experience, there will be a permanent place for you," he added.

Jenny sighed. It would be so easy to sit back and let her brothers take care of her. "I have my degree in business and I'd like to use it."

"There's plenty of other places to work in Dallas," Caroline offered. "Your daddy had numerous business contacts."

"No, Mom. I need to find my own way." Jenny pulled a piece of paper out of her pocket. "This came into the administration office on campus." She held her breath as her brothers read it.

LOOKING FOR A FRIENDLY,
CRIME-FREE COMMUNITY
WITH PLENTY OF BUSINESS AND JOB
OPPORTUNITIES? (ESPECIALLY FOR WOMEN)
PLEASE CONTACT MAYOR D. REILLY,
LAST HOPE, WY.

"Where the hell is this... Last Hope, Wyoming?" Brett asked.

"It's southwest of Gillette."

"All that's up there are coal mines and lots of snow."

"Not true. The town's growing and there are jobs."

"Says here they want *women*," Brett told her.

Jenny snatched the paper back. "It says they have *job opportunities* for women."

"Honey," Caroline said gently, "I don't think I like you going off to this strange town."

"You didn't stop Brett from going to Oklahoma, and he's only a few years older than I am," she stressed. "Don't you see? I want to experience what it's like to make it on my own. I want to meet that special someone and know what it's like to have a man care about me because of me, and not for my name or money. And I have two brothers who'll never accept the fact I've grown up."

She drew a deep breath. "If I'm ever going to have my own life, I'm going to have to leave Texas to get it."

Chapter One

Jenny Murdock hadn't expected to be greeted with a snowstorm in April. Her mouth fell open as big, puffy flakes landed against her windshield. This was impossible; it was nearly May. She hadn't packed any heavy clothes. Panic rose in her throat as she watched how rapidly the beautiful green landscape and the road up ahead disappeared under a blanket of white.

"Welcome to Wyoming," she murmured, fighting to keep her sports car on the road as strong winds whipped snow across the highway.

Reducing her speed, Jenny turned on the wipers and headlights. It didn't help much. She couldn't see more than three feet in front of her.

She glanced at her watch. It was nearly six o'clock. She couldn't be more than thirty minutes from Last Hope. Surely she could make it. All at once, the car began to slide. She eased her foot off the gas, but the traction was nil, and she had to pull over to the side of the road. Once stopped on the shoulder, she put the vehicle into park.

"Don't panic," she told herself as snow swirled around her. "Someone will be along any minute."

Feeling the temperature had dropped, she switched on the heater, then reached behind the seat for her denim jacket and put it on. Then she pushed the button on the radio to see if there was any weather information. Anxiously, she wiped the fog off the window and looked out, but it was no use, she couldn't see anything . . . or anyone else driving around in this weather.

She turned up the volume on the radio and listened to the weather advisory about the late-season blizzard.

Jenny closed her eyes and leaned back against the seat with a groan. For the first time, she began to doubt her decision.

"No, dammit!" She wouldn't allow herself any regrets. Opening her eyes, she sat up. "You just have to figure a way out of this mess."

Jenny looked at the gas gauge. It told her she had a quarter of a tank left. How long could she keep the engine running? There was a blanket in the trunk that would keep her warm until someone came. She shivered just thinking about getting out of the warm car, but she knew she had to make sure there wasn't anything blocking the exhaust pipe, allowing gas fumes into the car.

She snapped the closures on her jacket and tugged the collar up around her neck. After turning off the ignition, she pushed open the door and placed her foot on the ground. Ignoring the six inches of snow, burning cold and frigid wind, she made her way to the back of the car and quickly checked that there wasn't any snow around her exhaust pipe. Then she attempted to put the key into the trunk lock, but her fingers had been numbed by the cold.

As the key ring dropped, she watched it get swallowed up by the snow.

Luke Reilly drove his four-wheel-drive Bronco cautiously along the road next to the Double R. He was too tired, too hungry and too damn old to be out in weather like this. But if he hadn't moved his herd of cows and new calves into the corral, safe from the wicked storm, he might have lost them.

Luke had lived in northern Wyoming his entire life and knew all about these late-season storms. There wasn't a thing he could do but wait them out and hope they didn't do too much damage.

"Calling R One. You out there, Luke?"

Luke reached for his CB mike and pressed the button to talk to the sheriff. "Yeah, Tom, I'm crazy enough to be out in this." Luke had to fight the strong wind to keep the vehicle on the road.

"Well, you're not the only one. Old Charlie Owens called in saying he saw a red sports car pass by his place about an hour ago. It was having a rough time as it turned off on Old County Road 85. You anywhere near there? Over."

"Damn, crazy people, don't they know when to stay indoors?" Luke murmured. He wasn't that far away, but the last thing he wanted was to spend the night pulling people out of snow drifts. He sighed, knowing he could never leave man or beast out in this storm. "I'm about a mile or so from the turnoff. I'll go and see if I can spot a car."

"Thanks, Luke. That'll save me a long trip from town."

Luke pressed the button. "Do me a favor, Tom. Call the kids, and let 'em know I'll be delayed. Tell Crissy to go ahead with dinner." Luke's stomach reminded him he had skipped lunch.

"Sure will. Anything else?"

"Yeah, sweet-talk Molly into baking me one of her peach pies." He had known Tom and Molly Willis since he'd been a boy. Tom had been sheriff in the county for as long as Luke could remember.

"You got it. And thanks, Luke. Call me if you find anything. Over."

"This is R One. Over." Luke dropped the mike on the seat and began searching for the turnoff. It was slow going even with a four-wheel drive, so he wasn't doing anything fancy when he turned onto Old County Road. He wiped off the windshield with his gloved hand as he continued at a snail's pace along the snowpacked road, aware that he was quickly losing daylight. Then he saw something, a flash of color. Red. There was a red car parked on the shoulder.

He let his foot off the gas and coasted to a stop in the middle of the road, knowing the chances were good he could get stuck, too. He got out of the cab and trudged through the snow to the car. Pulling open the door, he found a woman huddled in the driver's seat.

"Oh, thank God!" she cried as she nearly jumped into his arms.

Luke had to smile as the grateful female clung to him. He wasn't used to this kind of attention. It had always been his brother who had the ladies falling all over him. "Hey, you okay?" He removed her cold fingers from around his neck.

The young woman blinked as if coming out of a trance, and he noticed how badly she was shivering. The inside of the car was nearly as cold as the outside, and what little clothing she had on was damp.

"I'm sorry," she managed to say as her body shook. "It's just...just that I'm so glad to see you. I've been here over an hour. I did...didn't think anyone was going to come along."

"Well, I'm here now. How about we get you to a warm, dry place?"

When she looked up at him with her big brown eyes, he felt a strange tightness in his chest. Something he hadn't felt in a long time. He didn't like it, either; he didn't like it at all. Scooping her up in his arms, Luke carried her to his truck and put her in the passenger side. Then he went back to her car and grabbed her purse, but couldn't find the keys. After locking the car, he raced around to the driver's side of the Bronco and hopped in. He turned up the heater full blast, then removed his sheepskin coat and wrapped it around his shivering passenger.

"You shouldn't have been out in this weather, especially in a vehicle without four-wheel drive. Where are your keys?"

"I lost them in the snow when I was trying to get a blanket out of the trunk."

"Well, we'll have to wait until the storm is over before we can look for them."

He picked up the CB mike and pressed the button. "R One, calling Sheriff One. Tom, you there?"

"Yeah, I'm here, son. What did you find?"

"The red car and a female inside. She's wet and cold. I'm taking her to the ranch."

"Any chance of hypothermia? Frostbite?"

Luke glanced at the small woman nearly buried in his coat. "Can you feel your fingers and toes?" he asked her.

She nodded. "They hurt."

"She's all right, Tom. Call you from the ranch. Over."

Ten minutes later, they reached the ranch house. It was completely dark now, but the porch light was on. Bless Crissy's heart for thinking about him. He honked, hurried around the Bronco and lifted his burden off the seat. She was light as a feather and very cooperative as she wrapped her arms around his neck. He carried her to the back door, which was now opened by his eleven-year-old daughter.

"What happened to the lady, Daddy?" she asked.

"Her car got stuck in the snow. She needs to get warm. Fast." He pushed his way through the kitchen. "Make a pot of coffee and some soup, honey," he instructed as he walked into the hall and started up the stairs.

Once in his room, he set her down on the bed and dashed into the connecting bathroom to turn on the hot water. Then he came back to get her.

"Okay, now let's get you out of those wet clothes."

Jenny Murdock used her hands to push off the bed, never taking her eyes off the tall, dark and very handsome stranger. Maybe she had been a little shook up from her ordeal, but surely this man didn't expect her to... just undress? With him watching? Before she knew what was happening, he was yanking off the coat he had put around her earlier and was picking her up. This time, he carried her into the steamy bathroom and stood her on the floor next to the tub.

"Now, can you manage to get undressed by yourself or do I need to do it for you?"

Suddenly, her temper flared. How dare he boss her around like some child. She placed her hands on her hips. "Where I come from, mister, we at least introduce ourselves before we get so familiar."

"Look, lady, there isn't time to play games. You need to get out of your wet clothes and bring your body temperature up." His hand shot out and grabbed her belt, yanking it off. Next, he sat her down on the toilet seat and started on her shoes.

"Okay. Okay!" Jenny jerked her foot out of his reach. "I can undress myself. But would you mind leaving? I'm a little shy about taking off my clothes in front of a stranger."

Jenny lay back in the tub and sighed as she sank lower into the warm water. Closing her eyes, she felt herself go liquid and tranquil. She had finally stopped shaking, but it was unlikely she would ever forget today's ordeal. Never in her life had she been so cold. Thank God he had stopped....

Jenny's eyes shot open. She didn't even know the man's name. The man who had rescued her, whose claw-footed bathtub she was soaking in. She glanced around the small bathroom to find an old-fashioned pedestal sink with a medicine cabinet overhead, the door open, displaying a lone razor and a can of shaving cream resting on a shelf. A chrome rod with two large maroon towels draped over it hung from one wall. She drew a long breath. There sure wasn't much here that told her anything about the fine-looking knight in shining armor.

A smile crossed her lips as she thought about her brothers. Boy, they would be having a fit right now if they knew she was in a strange man's bathtub.

She thought back to how Tyler and Brett had tried everything to stop her from leaving Aubrey, Texas, from promising never to interfere in her life again to Tyler bribing her with his new prize filly. It had taken nearly a month to convince her family that she meant business. And after receiving a positive reply to her résumé, Jenny knew that nothing or no one was going to stop her. And nothing had. Not a flat tire in Kansas, not a speeding ticket outside of Denver and not even an April blizzard in Wyoming. She had made it.

Now all she had on her mind was tomorrow morning's interview with Mayor Reilly.

A soft knock on the door made Jenny sit up and reach for a towel next to the tub. "Just a minute," she called out as she stood and quickly wrapped the big towel around her body. "Who is it?"

The door opened a crack and a blond-haired girl peered in. She had big blue eyes and a cute turned up nose. "My daddy said I should bring you a cup of coffee. But you looked cold so I made hot chocolate instead. Is that okay?"

Jenny smiled. "Oh, it's great. I love hot chocolate. Please come in."

The girl stepped from behind the door and walked inside. Her hair was in a ponytail, and she had a rich sprinkling of freckles across her nose. She was wearing a faded sweatshirt and worn jeans. Jenny guessed her age to be about eleven. She handed Jenny a stoneware mug with miniature marshmallows floating on top.

"Thank you." Jenny took a sip, then looked back at the girl who had been watching her closely. "Hi, I'm Jenny. What's your name?"

"I'm Crystal, but everyone calls me Crissy."

"Well, Crissy, I'm glad to meet you. I was even happier to meet your daddy when he rescued me from the blizzard.'' She sat down on the edge of the tub, adjusting the towel over her legs. "Too bad he wasn't able to rescue my suitcase, too.'' She glanced at Crissy. "Don't suppose your mother would have anything I might borrow until my clothes dry?''

"We don't have a mother.'' Another young voice came from the other side of the door.

"Go away, Garret,'' Crissy said as she went to the door and tried to shut it. "You're not supposed to see ladies without their clothes on.''

A small, dark-haired boy about five years old pushed his head through the slit in the door and looked at Jenny. "But she's not naked.''

Jenny almost choked on her chocolate. "It's okay, Crissy. I think this big towel is covering enough of me.'' She motioned the second child to enter. "Hi, I'm Jenny.''

"I'm Garret,'' the boy said. He was the opposite of his sister. His hair and coloring were dark and his build stockier. Like Crissy, he was wearing jeans and a sweatshirt. He was carrying some sort of toy figures. "You can't borrow our mama's clothes because she took them all when she went away. She's dead now.''

Although the little boy said this matter-of-factly, it didn't stop Jenny from feeling the big tug on her heart.

"I'm so sorry.'' She looked from brother to sister. They both seemed adjusted to the idea. Not Jenny. It had been over two years since her father's death, she still wasn't used to the idea. She doubted she ever would be. "You must miss her a lot.''

Crissy's eyes looked downward, and she didn't say anything.

The boy tipped his head to the side. "I don't remember her much, and my daddy doesn't like to talk about her. He says we don't need a foolish, no-sense woman around here anyway. We can get along just fine by ourselves.'' Garret studied her for a moment. "Are you a foolish, no-sense woman, too?''

Jenny stiffened. How dare that man teach his son such rot. "I have plenty of sense, Garret. I just happened to get caught by a freak snowstorm. Where I come from, we don't get snow in the spring."

The boy's big brown eyes lit up, and Jenny realized he looked a lot like his father. "We do. Sometimes we get it in June. Where ya from?"

"Dallas, Texas. But I might be living here, so it's a good thing you told me. Now I'll be prepared. I'll also need to thank your daddy for being around to help me."

"You're going to move to Last Hope?" Crissy asked, her eyes expressing her surprise.

Jenny took another sip of her hot drink. "I have a job interview tomorrow. If I can make it into town."

"You're not going to make it anywhere for the next few days." Jenny recognized the deep voice before she looked up to see her rescuer appear.

The small bathroom sure was getting crowded, she thought as the six-foot-plus man with broad shoulders filled the doorway. Thick black hair lay in waves across his forehead. His chiseled jaw was tense and his chocolate-colored deep-set eyes were unreadable. He was wearing a plaid flannel shirt and a pair of faded jeans that fit narrow hips and long muscular legs. He was absolutely gorgeous.

"Looks like you're stuck here at least through tomorrow."

His words brought Jenny out of her reverie, and she stood. "But I have to be in Last Hope tomorrow morning," she argued. The knot in the towel didn't hold with her quick movement and the material began to slip. She grabbed it, preventing a humiliating disaster. Regaining her composure, she glanced up to find the stranger's gaze on her hands. Her skin began to tingle from his heated stare, but she ignored the sensation. She had other problems to worry about.

"Do you at least have something I can wear?" she asked.

Crissy and Garret looked up at their father. Jenny could tell they both thought he walked on water.

He pulled a navy robe from behind the door and handed it to her. "Here, put this on." Then his gaze traveled the entire length of her body. Darn it! There went the tingling again.

"I'll see what else I can rustle up," he added after a moment.

"Crissy, go see if you have anything she can borrow, and Garret you go with her."

Both children hurried out of the room. Jenny wanted to call them back. Maybe she was small, but she didn't think she could fit into little Crissy's clothes.

"I'll go see what I have," he told her, then started out the door.

"Wait, can't you just go and get my suitcase? I really have an important appointment tomorrow."

He braced his arm against the doorjamb. "Take a look outside, lady. There's no way I can get two feet from the house, let alone the two miles to your car. You don't know how lucky you are that I found you when I did, or you would have a helluva lot more to worry about than finding something stylish to wear."

Suddenly, she was ashamed. This man had probably saved her life, and he had opened his home to her. Whether he was friendly or not, she had to make the best of the situation. "I apologize. I never thanked you for rescuing me. And it's very kind of you to take me into your home, Mr... I'm sorry, I don't even know your name. I'm Jenny Murdock." She offered him her hand.

The stranger just looked at it, and said, "Luke Reilly."

Jenny froze, then her pulse began to race. "Reilly?"

He nodded.

"You're... you're the mayor of Last Hope?"

"No, that's my brother, Drew." He watched her for a few seconds, then a mischievous smile worked its way across his face. "Don't tell me your appointment is with him?"

From the numerous phone conversations she'd had with the mayor, she couldn't imagine the man standing before her being related to him. "Yes, I'm seeing Mayor Reilly tomorrow for a job interview." Jenny had already been offered the job, but she wanted to meet the man and look the town over before accepting the position as administrative assistant.

"I should have guessed." He shook his head and began to grin. "You're one of Reilly's brides."

Chapter Two

"What do you mean, one of Reilly's brides?"

Luke studied the near-naked woman standing in front of him, while his body reminded him it had been a long time since any female had shared his bed or bath. She had folded her arms under her breasts, letting him know that they were full and round, just the size to fit his hands. The thought made his palms itch. He released a long, slow breath and raised his gaze to her face.

Dammit! The last thing he needed was Jenny Murdock flashing her big brown eyes at him. He didn't need any woman in his life, especially one looking for a husband.

He shrugged. "It's just a nickname a few people have given to Drew's idea of recruiting women in his life."

"I assure you, Mr. Reilly, I'm here to interview for the position of administrative assistant," she stressed. "Although I...I see nothing wrong with women wanting to get married, I have no immediate plans."

"So...you're saying that you moved all the way up here from Texas just to answer an ad in the paper for an administrative assistant?'' Luke asked as he folded his arms across his chest.

She nodded. ''Just as I told you before, I have an interview scheduled with the mayor first thing in the morning.''

''And that's the only reason you came here?''

Luke watched the little brunette's back straighten and her eyes flash. He could tell by her stylish haircut and her manicured nails that she was the kind of woman used to having nice things. She was way out of his league.

''I wanted a change of scenery, Mr. Reilly. I've lived in Texas all my life and wanted a change.''

''Well, this is beautiful country, but watch your step, Ms. Murdock,'' he warned, all the time wondering if her hair was as soft as it looked. ''The men in these parts work hard, and a lot of them like to play hard, too. You might find out that you bit off more than you can chew.'' With that, he turned and left the room.

Jenny stared at Luke as he walked away. If she didn't know better, she would say her brother Tyler had hired this man to irritate her so she would go back home. Well, she wasn't going to let a man dictate to her. Not anymore.

She shut the bathroom door and let the towel drop to the floor. Slipping into the large robe, she tied the belt around her waist, but it wasn't much help keeping the lapels together.

''And what's wrong with looking for a husband?'' she said quietly. ''Why does it always have to be the man who makes the first move?'' She rolled up the sleeves and managed to find her hands. ''Darn it! When and if I decide to look for a husband, it's my business, no one else's,'' she added. She started to walk and tripped over the hem, nearly falling down. *I'm definitely going to look for a man who's under giant size,* she thought. She'd grabbed fistfuls of robe and was holding it up as the door swung open, and Luke came in.

''I found these things...'' His words drifted off as his gaze fell to her legs.

Jenny glanced down and realized the front of the robe was open all the way up her thighs. She quickly dropped the terry cloth and reached for the clothes he was holding out.

"What did you find?" She tried to hide her disappointment when she discovered the large pair of sweats and a T-shirt that had to be his, and a pair of white cotton underpants that had to be his daughter's.

"Sorry, it was all I could round up," he said. "Anything else you need will have to wait until your clothes get washed." He bent down and grabbed her stack of wet things, including her lacy bra and matching panties. "I'll have Crissy put these in the washer."

Jenny felt the situation was entirely too imitate, but there wasn't anything she could do. "Thank you."

He nodded. "After you get dressed, come downstairs for something to eat. It isn't much, canned soup and lunch-meat sandwiches."

"Sounds wonderful," Jenny said as she brushed back her shoulder-length hair. "Give me a little time to put these on." She looked up to find him studying her and was entranced by his dark, smoldering gaze. Then, she quickly glanced away. "Well, thanks again for the clothes."

Luke nodded and walked out. Jenny shut the door again, but this time she locked it.

"Why can't she stay here, Dad?" Garret asked. He sat at the kitchen table, his toy figures laid out in front of him. "Jenny said she wants a job. Can't we be her job?"

Luke carried the soup from the stove and poured it into the bowl. He didn't like the way this conversation was going. "She's already interviewing for a job in town, son. And I don't think she wants to be a housekeeper."

"Why?" He picked up one of his Power Rangers figures. "We're good. I don't make a mess."

"Son, some people like to do other kinds of jobs besides cooking and chasing after two kids."

Garrett looked thoughtful. "Like when you wanted to work on the ranch, not in the coal mines anymore?"

Luke was taken aback. He'd quit his job at the mines nearly two years ago. How could his son remember? "Yeah, kind of like that."

"But, can we just ask her?" Garrett persisted. "She's really pretty. Huh, Dad, don't you think Jenny's really pretty?"

Luke rubbed the back of his neck. He was too tired for this tonight, especially since he'd been up early preparing for the storm. "Yeah, son, she's pretty."

He called Crissy to the table, hoping for a change of subject.

"I put Jenny's clothes in the washer," the eleven-year-old said as she took her seat at the table. "Oh, Daddy, her jeans are just the kind I want."

Luke knew where this was leading. "You've got plenty of jeans."

"But all the girls..." Crissy's argument died when Luke gave her the end-of-discussion look. She started eating her soup.

Luke sighed quietly, knowing that his daughter's teenage years were approaching, and he wouldn't get off so easily. He watched her quietly eating. She was turning into a lovely girl, and he knew that before long he would have a tough time keeping the boys in line.

Crissy was like her mother in that respect. Luke hoped that beauty was all his daughter had inherited from Cynthia Reilly.

"I guess some of your pants are getting too short," he began. "Maybe the next time we go into town, we can look for a pair of those jeans."

Crissy smiled. "Thanks, Daddy."

"What about me?" Garrett asked. "Can I get some more Power Rangers?"

"I know what Power Rangers are. My nephew has some."

Everyone turned to find Jenny standing in the doorway. She was wearing his gray sweats, the pants rolled up several times. The shirt nearly hung to her knees, and a pair of white socks covered her small feet. Her hair was in a braid, but soft curls circled her heart-shaped face.

Damn, she looked good. He got up, nodded to the seat next to Crissy and went to the stove as Garrett began questioning Jenny.

"Is your nephew five, too?" Garrett asked.

"No, he's only three and a half, but he has all the Power Ranger figures. He even sleeps with them."

"So does Garrett," Crissy volunteered.

"I do not," the boy denied. "I was just playing with them and got tired."

"Yeah, sure," Crissy said. "Like every night."

Garrett got up on his knees. "Well, at least I don't write dumb stuff in a book and hide it under my bed."

"You better stay away from my diary," Crissy said as tears threatened in her eyes.

Luke raised a hand. "That's enough, you two. We have a guest."

Jenny smiled as she leaned back in her chair. "Gosh, I feel like I'm at home."

"You have brothers and sisters?" Garrett asked.

"I have two big brothers." She glanced at Luke. "Really big and *very* protective."

Luke poured some soup into her bowl, then looked her in the eyes. "Is that a warning, Ms. Murdock?"

Jenny's eyes locked with Luke's challenging glare. Why did this man make her feel as if they were playing tug-of-war? "I'm just stating a fact, Mr. Reilly." That wasn't the half of it, Jenny thought, knowing too well how Tyler treated any male interested in his kid sister.

"You got any brothers my age?" Garrett asked, apparently oblivious to what was going on between her and his father.

"No, Garrett. Tyler and Brett are grown-up and married. I do have a niece, but she's almost twelve, and my two nephews are three and a half and six months old." She smiled. Already she missed them. "Sorry."

The boy's expression was bleak. "I never have anyone to play with."

Jenny looked at Luke and arched an eyebrow.

"Garrett doesn't start school until the fall," he said as he sat down. "Our closest neighbor is over six miles away, so there aren't any kids his age around."

For the first time, Jenny saw compassion in the man's eyes. So he wasn't the hard-nose he pretended to be, not with his kids, anyway. "Well, Garrett, I know I'm a little old, but since I'm going to be staying here tonight, maybe I can play with you. Board games, card games . . . whatever you want."

"Power Rangers."

"Sure, there's a girl Power Ranger." Then her attention went to Crissy. "And maybe we can play something, too."

The young girl shook her head. "Oh, I'm too old to play games."

"Well, I'm just going to have to change your mind. Do you have a Monopoly game? A deck of cards?"

"I have Go Fish," Garrett offered.

"Good, we can play that, too. But we have to finish supper and clean up the kitchen."

"But I'm too young to do the dishes," Garrett said.

Jenny bit back a grin. "Well, Garrett, you look pretty big to me. I bet you could sweep the floor and help carry the dishes to the sink. I used to do that when I was your age."

"I can do that," the boy answered. "Can we play Go Fish first?"

Jenny picked up her spoon. "Sure. I just need to make a phone call after dinner. My family is probably worried." She looked at Luke. "Do you think we could call your brother, too, and let him know that I'll be delayed tomorrow?"

Luke shook his head. "Can't make any calls tonight. The storm knocked out the lines."

As if to reinforce Luke's statement, the wind whistled outside the kitchen window and the lights flickered. Jenny shivered. "Does this happen often?"

"This is northern Wyoming, we have long winters here," Luke said. "But don't worry, we have plenty of wood for the fireplace if the electricity goes out and we can't run the heater."

Jenny didn't like being isolated, and obviously the man across from her didn't like it any better than she did. Heaven forbid if her brothers found out she was about to spend the night with a stranger.

An hour later, Luke was pacing the living room. Every so often, he stopped at the window to check the weather conditions, wondering how many calves he would lose if this storm didn't die out by morning. He had a good herd this year and had been looking forward to spring roundup in two weeks. After the last three years of just scraping by, he had spent pretty close to the rest of his savings to increase the size of his herd. These new calves were supposed to be the big payoff.

He glanced outside again, not even able to see the barn. Damn! Mother Nature sure could make a mess of things.

Suddenly, ripples of laughter from the other room invaded his thoughts. The sound of his kids' voices made Luke smile despite his problems. Over the past few years, they hadn't had a whole lot to be happy about. Garrett had been barely two, but Crissy had been old enough to remember her mother taking off. Luke still wasn't able to forgive Cindy for abandoning her children.

His fists clenched, remembering the day his wife walked out. Suitcases in hand, tears in her eyes, she told him that she couldn't live the life he wanted her to. She needed to go away to find herself.

Luke shook his head, studying the blowing snow. Since the day they had married, he'd catered to Cindy's every whim, and in the process had nearly lost the family ranch when she wanted him to move into town and go to work in the mines. And still none of that made her happy. Not the extra money, not the kids and sure as hell not him.

When he found out about the other men, he decided he'd had enough and brought the children back to the ranch. She followed, begging him to take her back, swearing that it would never happen again. He'd believed her. Six months later, she found another lover and was off to California. Immediately, he filed for divorce and custody of Crissy and Garrett. Thank God, the kids had never become an issue. Long before they were to go to court, Cindy was killed in a traffic accident in Los Angeles. Although his love for his wife had faded with her infidelities, he never wished her harm.

More laughter from the other room drew his attention to the woman causing all the merriment. Jenny Murdock. No! He wouldn't let his kids get attached to someone who wasn't going to stick around. Jenny was here to find a husband. He would bet a dozen of his newborn calves she was looking for one with money, too. Well, he didn't have money, and he definitely wasn't husband material. But that didn't stop him from noticing that she had big coffee-colored eyes, full, pouty lips and the shapeliest pair of legs he had ever seen. His body stirred to life. It had been a very long time.

"Daddy, Daddy," Garrett called out.

Luke added another log to the fire and closed the screen, then went into the dining room to see what his children and houseguest were up to.

"You want to play Monopoly, Daddy?" his son asked. "Jenny said if you help me, we can play girls against boys."

Luke caught the gleam in Ms. Murdock's eyes. She was challenging him. "Sure, why not?"

* * *

Two hours later, Garrett was sitting on his father's lap, trying hard to keep his eyes open. Jenny glanced at the antique grandfather clock against the wall. It was nearly ten o'clock.

Even Crissy, who had been an admirable partner, had faded in the last thirty minutes. She glanced at Luke. He didn't look sleepy at all, he acted as if he could play the game all night.

"I think it's time to stop. The players are dropping like flies," she said.

Luke looked down at his son. "Yeah, guess it's bedtime."

Garrett started to protest but soon gave in when his father tucked him against his broad shoulder and stood up from the oak table. Jenny watched as the large man walked across the room to the staircase. Grabbing the railing, he maneuvered the stairs with ease.

Jenny turned to Crissy. "Why don't we leave this and finish the game tomorrow?"

The young girl's eyes lit up. "Yeah, there won't be any school tomorrow with the snow."

"I bet you're really unhappy about that," Jenny teased.

"Oh, I like school, but that's because there's nobody here, except for Garrett."

Jenny quickly realized that there wasn't another adult at the ranch. "But who watches you and your brother?"

"We've had housekeepers. Marge was our favorite, but she got married and moved into town."

"Who watches Garrett when you're in school?" Surely the man didn't leave a five-year-old alone, she thought.

"Dad does."

"But what about the ranch?"

"I can handle both," a familiar male voice said.

Jenny turned around to find Luke had returned. "I'm sorry, I didn't mean to imply that you couldn't." She felt her checks redden. "I was just curious to know how you handled a ranch and two children."

Luke looked at his daughter. "Crissy, please go put some sheets on the bed in the guest room. Then I think you should hit the sack, too."

Crissy started to speak, but changed her mind. Instead, she kissed her father on the cheek and then turned to Jenny. "Good night, Jenny."

"Good night, Crissy. See you in the morning."

The girl nodded then hurried up the steps. When she disappeared, Jenny noticed that Luke was staring at her.

"Maybe I should go up, too, and help Crissy with the bed," she said. She started to leave, but Luke grabbed her arm to stop her.

"Just so you'll know, I handle the ranch and my family just fine, Ms. Murdock."

Jenny swallowed hard. The last thing she wanted was to tangle with this man anymore tonight.

Luke had other ideas. "I don't need some stranger butting into something that's none of her business. Believe me, I take a helluva lot better care of my kids than their mother ever did." His jaw tensed, his dark eyes remained cold and hard. "And if you've got any ideas about my needing a partner to help around here, think again. I'm not the kind of man you want to get mixed up with. I'm the wrong Reilly." With that, he released her and marched out of the room.

Jenny watched the snow from the bedroom window, wondering if it was ever going to stop. The question most on her mind was how long would she be stuck here? She knew Luke Reilly wanted her out of his house as soon as possible, which suited her just fine. She didn't need a grumpy male in her life, anyway.

She turned away from the window and walked to the comfortable-looking double bed and the handmade quilt lying across the top. It would probably keep her nice and warm tonight. She glanced around the room at the floral wallpaper and bare hardwood floors, partially covered with a braided rug. Jenny felt as if she'd stepped back in time. Although she wasn't an expert, she knew a lot of the furnishings were antiques. She went to the dresser and ran her hand over the mahogany, recalling the beautiful oak trestle table in the dining room. She wouldn't mind living in a big old house like this.

Her thoughts turned to the sullen man who occupied the premises. He'd reminded her a lot of her brother Tyler. Angry at the world, or just at the women who accidentally came into his life. Well, she didn't want to be here any more than he wanted her here. And as soon as the roads were cleared, she was out of here.

Just then, there was a knock on the door, and Jenny quickly answered it. She found Luke standing in the hallway. His shirt was unbuttoned and pulled out of his jeans; underneath he wore a gray thermal undershirt, showing off a broad chest. Did the man have to look so damn sexy all the time?

He held up a white T-shirt. "I thought you might need something to sleep in."

Jenny felt uncomfortable with his stare. "Thank you. I get pretty cold at night."

"I'm just the opposite. I don't wear much, I get too...hot—" His voice broke off. "I can get you another blanket if you need it."

"No, I'll be fine. I'll just wear socks and your shirt," she said. Luke nodded and continued to stand there looking at her. "Is there something else...?" she asked.

He glanced away, but his gaze came back to her. "Look, about what I said earlier...I'm sorry. I haven't been around women much lately. I guess I lost my manners."

"No, you had every right, I was asking personal questions," Jenny admitted. "But believe me, I wasn't criticizing. I was just curious to know how you were a single parent and still managed to run a ranch."

"I don't know." He shrugged. "I get up every morning and just do it. I have pretty good kids, and Crissy helps a lot. We tried housekeepers, but the ones I've found don't like living so far from town.''

Jenny relaxed her grip on the doorknob. ''What about Marge?''

Luke actually smiled. ''She was great with the kids, and they loved her. But another man recognized her good qualities and married her.''

Jenny blinked. ''She chose another man over you?''

Luke looked taken aback at her question. ''Oh, no. Marge and I never ... we never ... Jenny, Marge was fifty-five.''

All of a sudden, they both began to laugh. For the first time since she'd arrived, she felt relaxed with this man.

''Single women don't last long around this area.'' He was still smiling and Jenny was mesmerized by it. ''That should be good for you. You should find a husband easily, especially since you're so pretty.''

Jenny's heart took a tumble. ''I think you found your manners, Mr. Reilly.''

He moved closer to her, his head dipped, placing his mouth only inches from hers. ''Lady, you wouldn't say that if you knew what was on my mind right now.''

Chapter Three

The next morning, Jenny rolled over in bed and opened her eyes. It took a minute or two to get her bearings and realize she wasn't in her own bed. She wasn't even in her own house. Throwing back the covers, she got up and went to the window, hoping that all the snow had miraculously melted and the sun had come out. She pulled back the curtains. Ice had built up on the glass. She couldn't see anything. This wasn't good, she thought, suddenly feeling a chill against her skin. She put on her sweats and hurried out the door. Her journey was shortened when she collided with Luke in the hall.

"Whoa." He grabbed hold of her arms to steady her. "Where are you headed in such an all-fired hurry so early in the morning?"

Jenny tipped her head back to gaze into a pair of rich brown eyes. Her attention quickly moved to the dark stubble along his square jaw. She inhaled his familiar smell, an intoxicating mixture of soap and his own manly scent. She glanced at his cheeks and noticed a ruddy hue. He must have already been outside.

"I...I wanted to see if it was still snowing." She combed her hair back. "My window has ice on it."

"The snow stopped, but it's mighty cold. The windchill factor is probably near zero."

"Well, that's good if the snow has stopped. Pretty soon the snowplow will come by, and I can get my car."

Luke couldn't help staring at Jenny. Her ivory skin was flushed and only a small crease marred her flawless cheek. She blinked the sleep from her eyes, her soft, pouty mouth beckoning to him all the time. He glanced away. "There's a lot of snow out there. So it'll be a while before we can get to your car."

"What about the phone? Is it working?"

"I doubt it. The telephone repairmen usually don't get out until the roads have been plowed."

"What do we do until then?"

Luke could think of a lot things he wanted to do with Ms. Murdock to pass the time, but the memory of another woman who nearly destroyed him helped him dismiss his carnal thoughts.

"We could have breakfast," he suggested as he rubbed his cold hands together. "C'mon to the kitchen, I've got the oven going."

Jenny nodded and followed Luke downstairs.

The big old kitchen had always been the warmest spot in the house. And with the huge oven door partially open, the heat had swiftly circulated throughout the room. He smiled as Jenny stood in front of the oven, allowing the intense heat to warm her hands, then her backside.

"You know you'll have to get used to the cold if you're going to live in northern Wyoming."

"I can handle the cold." She straightened. "I just hadn't expected to be greeted with snow in April."

"Well, you better plan on it, because these storms are common."

Jenny sat down at the table. "I will."

He handed her a cup of coffee. "Here, this should help warm you."

"Thanks." Jenny took the mug and quickly took a sip. "Mmm... This is good."

Damn! Did she have to enjoy everything with so much...enthusiasm? he thought, recalling the Monopoly game last night and the teasing glint in her eyes every time she had collected rent from him. He scraped back his chair, got up and went to the refrigerator. "How do you like your eggs?"

"Scrambled." Jenny stood, moved to the stove and placed a cast-iron skillet on the front burner. "But, I'll cook. How do you like your eggs?"

Luke wasn't about to argue. It had been a long time since someone other than Crissy handled the kitchen duties. "Scrambled is fine."

Jenny pushed the big sleeves up her arms and just as quickly they slid down again. However, it didn't seem to hamper her from her work. While turning six strips of bacon on the back griddle, she used the other hand to expertly crack eggs into a bowl.

She glanced in his direction. "I worked in a diner one summer when I was in college."

Next, she walked to the refrigerator. Luke felt his heart race as Jenny bent over to get a better look inside, causing her sweatpants to pull tight over her curvy little bottom.

Without straightening, Jenny swung her head around and smiled. "Do you know you have fuzzy things growing in your vegetable bin?"

He blinked. "Huh? What do you need from there?"

"I wanted to make a Mexican omelet."

"Don't bother, it's too much trouble. I'll just pour some salsa over my eggs." He wasn't sure he wanted her to get so familiar with his kitchen.

"But I like to cook."

"Another good quality." He leaned against the counter, eyeing her closely. "Gosh, Ms. Murdock, you're just chock-full of domestic talent. You should have no trouble at all finding a husband.''

Jenny rested her arm on the door. What was wrong with him? One minute he seemed friendly, the next she got the feeling he wanted to toss her out in the snow. ''You act like I'm going to be put on an auction block and go to the highest bidder.''

''In Last Hope, that's highly possible,'' he answered. ''There are a lot of lonely miners looking for wives to come home to. In fact, one of my brother's campaign promises was to bring economic growth to Last Hope. He's also looking for marriageable-age women.''

Jenny walked back to the stove and concentrated on breakfast. ''There is nothing wrong with that. Haven't you ever been lonely, Luke? Living out here, so far from town, so far from other people.''

Hell, yes, he'd been lonely. Some nights he ached from it. ''Maybe I like being all alone. I sure as hell have gotten used to it.''

She looked up at him. Her eyes seemed to reach deep inside him. ''Luke, no one ever gets used to being alone.''

He glanced away, but it didn't help. He was already drawn to her...her smell...her smile...her voice. Damn! Her husky voice. It was like the woman was under his skin, and he couldn't get her out. No! He had to fight it.

''Sometimes we're not given a choice. We just have to take the cards we're dealt.''

Suddenly, Garrett appeared in the doorway. ''Are we going to play cards some more?''

The interruption was a relief to Luke. ''Not right now, son.'' He looked at the boy still in pajamas. ''Why aren't you dressed?''

'' 'Cause my clean clothes are down here.''

Luke went into the utility room off the kitchen and came back with a stack of clean jeans and shirts. ''Here, take these up to your room.''

The child didn't move. ''Can I eat first?''

Luke was about to argue, but the last thing he wanted was to be alone with Ms. Murdock. "Sure, you want a bowl of your favorite cereal?"

Garrett tossed one of his million-dollar smiles Jenny's way. "No, I want some eggs."

"Since when do you eat eggs?"

"You burn them, Dad," Garrett explained as he placed his Power Rangers figures on the table, then sat down.

Luke caught Jenny's grin, which made him angry. So he wasn't the greatest cook. He had done the best he could. He studied his stocky-built son. It sure didn't look as if the boy had suffered.

"Fine, you eat eggs." Luke walked to the back door and grabbed his coat off the hook, then put on his hat. "I'm going to the barn and check the horses."

"But what about your breakfast?" Jenny asked.

"I don't have much of an appetite." He opened the door, bracing himself against the strong wind as he walked out, then slammed it behind him.

Jenny bit her lip. What had gotten into him? she wondered. She looked out the window and saw Luke carefully walking along the freshly shoveled path to the big red barn. Her gaze traveled to the fenced corral and another smaller structure. She raised her eyes to the beautiful snowcapped mountains in the distance. She sighed. It wouldn't take much to get used to this, she thought.

"Where's my daddy?" Crissy asked as she came into the kitchen.

"He's feeding the stock, honey," Jenny said. "I'm fixing breakfast. Bacon and eggs."

The girl didn't act too excited. She seemed more concerned about her father. "He isn't going to go out and check the calves, is he?"

"No, I think he's just going to the barn."

"Is he coming back soon?"

"Crissy, don't worry, he just went out to feed the stock. I don't know how many animals you have in the barn, honey, but I'm sure he'll be back before too long."

"We have five horses and a pony," Crissy said.

"The pony is mine," Garrett volunteered. "His name is Willie. But next year I'll be old enough to ride a horse."

"Only if you can take care of him," the girl warned.

"I can, Daddy showed me how."

"But you have to do it all the time."

"I will," he promised.

Crissy placed her hands on her hips. "Like you clean your room?"

"I don't like to clean my room, but I like taking care of horses."

"But you have to do both."

"Whoa, you two," Jenny said, raising her hand. "Why don't we eat, then clean up the kitchen and your bedrooms? And maybe later we can finish the Monopoly game."

They both cheered up and Jenny glanced out the window. "Hopefully by then your father will be back," she mumbled, eyeing the trail to the barn.

Luke tossed the pail next to the feed bin. Damn! What had gotten into him? He leaned against the stall and watched the pony eat. Suddenly, his pretty houseguest came to mind. Who would have thought that a woman could look so damn inviting at six in the morning? Her chestnut hair all curly and wild, her face flushed with sleep.

At least she'd slept. He had stared at the ceiling most of the night. Some of his restlessness had been caused by the storm and his concern for the new calves, but it was Jenny Murdock who had managed to occupy his mind in the quiet hours before dawn. Her presence in the house was a painful reminder that he hadn't shared a woman's company in a long time, and a helluva lot longer than that since he'd had one in his bed.

Restless, Luke strolled down the row of stalls to check on the roan mare, Sassy Girl. She was due to foal next month. With any luck, her colt would help stock his new riding-stable business. Already he was boarding three horses. But in the next two years, he wanted to build another barn and corral.

The Double R Ranch backed up toward the Big Horn Mountains and had some of the most beautiful scenery in the state of Wyoming. And Luke loved every square inch of this land. Drew had never felt that way.

Luke had been twelve and Drew only nine when their mother passed away. Because his brother was so young, he'd been sent to live with an aunt and uncle in town. Luke had stayed with his father, Michael, and had helped work the ranch. He and Drew had never been close. They were too different.

Luke only saw Drew on holidays. Ranching was a hard life, especially in the winter. While Luke was riding around nearly sixty thousand acres and learning how to hunt elk and antelope, Drew was involved in school and worrying about where to go to college.

Luke was happy for his younger brother until Drew returned to Last Hope after Michael's death and decided he wanted to sell his share of the ranch. Luckily, their daddy's will stated that the brothers couldn't sell just half the ranch. They both had to agree. And as long as Luke had breath left in his body, he never would.

He absently rubbed the mare's dark muzzle, and she raised her head to get more attention. He smiled. "You females are all alike. You always want more."

"Maybe it's because you men give so little."

Luke spun around. Jenny was wearing her jeans and blouse from yesterday. One of his heavy jackets partially swallowed her up. He glanced at her feet and noticed that she had on a pair of Crissy's boots. "What are you doing out here?"

She rested her hands on her hips. "It's been nearly two hours, and you never returned. Your daughter is worried that something happened to you."

"Sorry, I just wanted to get some air." He turned away. "You better go inside before you catch cold."

Jenny ignored him and went to the mare. "She's pretty." She climbed onto the railing. "When is she due to foal?"

"Next month."

Luke watched her easy manner around the skittish animal as she rubbed Sassy's nose. "You say your brother breeds horses."

"Quarter horses. I've been mucking out stalls for as long as I can remember." She turned to him and smiled. "But I never minded. They're such beautiful animals. They say dogs are loyal, but I think a good horse is more so."

"Do you have one?"

"Yeah, Old Glory. She's getting up there in years, but she's a great horse. I'm going to miss her."

"You can always come here and ride." Luke was surprised at his offer. "I don't have any Thoroughbreds, but they're all good saddle horses."

She looked up at him in surprise. "Oh, Luke. That's so nice of you." All at once, she hopped off the railing and threw her arms around him.

There were too many clothes between them for the hug to be intimate. But that didn't change the fact that Luke didn't want to let Jenny go, not yet. When she started to pull away, he gripped her arms, holding her close. They both froze. Then her eyes widened, her lips parting as if just waiting for him... Luke didn't stop to think, he bent his head and took what she was offering.

The first touch was soft, and he felt her tremble. Or was it him? His eyes drifted shut as he pulled her into his arms and pressed his mouth against hers, savoring the sweetness. It wasn't long before the hunger intensified with the kiss. Jenny released a soft moan and her hands circled his neck, her fingers combing through his hair, sending shivers down his spine.

Dear Lord, this woman was dangerous. He continued to take nibbling bites from her sensuous mouth, then slipped his tongue inside. He groaned and pressed her against the stall railing. He wanted her.

"Daddy! Where are you?"

Hearing Crissy's voice, they jumped apart. "We're over here," Luke called hoarsely.

His daughter appeared, her gaze wandering from one to the other. "The phone is working and Uncle Drew called. Sheriff Tom told him about Jenny staying here. He said to tell you that he's going to get Jenny's car towed and not to worry, that he would drive out and get her this afternoon."

Luke didn't know who he was most angry with—himself or his brother. "Thanks, Crissy," he muttered, his eyes on Jenny's kiss-swollen lips. "Looks like you're getting rescued. And just in time."

Several hours later, after cleaning up the kitchen and helping the kids make their beds, Jenny sat at the table playing Go Fish with Crissy and Garrett.

"This is a dumb game," Crissy said, holding her fish-shaped cards in her hands.

"Is not," Garrett argued. "You're just mad because you're not winning."

"I am not!" Crissy shouted.

"Are, too—"

"Hey, kids, I'm going to stop playing if you can't behave," Jenny threatened. Being cooped up in the house was hard on all of them. Except for Luke. He had gone out again after lunch and hadn't returned yet.

"I don't care," Crissy said. "I don't want to play anymore." She tossed her cards down.

"Okay, we'll do something else," Jenny suggested, but she was getting restless, as well. She got up from the table and looked out the kitchen window. The threatening gray clouds overhead made for a gloomy day, and the weather was reflected in everyone's mood. At least she'd gotten to phone her mother and had let her know that she was all right. Thank goodness, Tyler was away, because Jenny hadn't had the energy for another argument. She sighed tiredly and walked out of the kitchen, leaving the children to clean up the card game.

She wandered into the large living room and smiled at the comfortable-looking dark green sofa and the two rust-colored chairs arranged in front of the stone hearth. The hardwood floors were well-kept, but dull with dust. The area rug had worn spots, one in particular was in front of the television. Her gaze moved to the maple deacon's bench against the wall. Next to it was a beautiful Windsor chair.

She walked to the other side of the room and the small alcove that held a large mahogany desk. The top was covered with papers and books, but it didn't hide the beautifully preserved piece. Did Luke have any idea he possessed a houseful of priceless antiques?

The big clock over the mantel chimed. It was already two o'clock. Jenny couldn't believe it. A little over twenty-four hours had passed since she had crossed the Wyoming state line and already so much had happened to her. Her heart began to race as her fingers touched her mouth.

Perhaps the best part was being kissed...kissed as she had never been kissed before.

"If you're checking my assets, Ms. Murdock, I'm afraid that you're not going to find much."

Jenny jerked around to see Luke standing in the arched doorway. His long muscular legs were braced apart and his arms were folded across his broad chest.

She felt her cheeks redden. "I was just admiring the desk. You have some beautiful antiques."

He cocked an eyebrow. "Oh, yeah?"

Jenny's gaze went to his forearms, unable to keep herself from remembering how tightly they had held her only a few hours ago.

She looked up and caught his brooding expression, and her anger began to build. "I'm sorry if you thought I was snooping. Maybe I should have waited in my room until your brother comes to get me. But I thought it would be nice if I occupied the kids for a while, since you seem to be disappearing a lot."

"I have a ranch to run," he countered.

"You also have two small children to raise."

He placed his hands on his hips. "I've managed so far on my own."

"The key word here is *you've* managed. They haven't." Jenny saw him flinch and almost felt sorry for him. "They're lonely, Luke."

Luke drew a deep breath and released it. He didn't need this woman coming in here and analyzing him or his kids. It was none of her business, anyway. Did he ask to be the one to find her stranded in the snow? "They have each other."

"But what about when Crissy goes back to school?"

Luke stepped closer, but it didn't seem to intimidate her at all. "Look, there isn't much I can do. My dad had to raise me the same way after my mother died. Hell, don't you think I know it gets lonely?" He stared into her eyes and saw a flash of compassion. He had to turn away. Damn! She had him so confused, he didn't know if he wanted to throw her out of his home or drag her into his arms again and kiss her senseless.

"It's different here in Wyoming. We're pretty much isolated during the winter," he said talking over his shoulder. "The weather can be brutal. Maybe you better think twice before you decide to stay."

The room was silent for so long he thought she'd left, then he felt her hand touch him on his back. "I'm sorry, Luke," she said in a husky voice that tugged all the right strings. He fought hard to keep from facing her.

"I had no right to criticize how you're raising your kids," she went on. "I just thought it would be better if you had someone to stay with them. You know...like a house-keeper, or something."

Slowly, he turned. "Like I told you, the housekeepers I found didn't like being so far away from town."

She frowned. "It's not that far. What, about twenty-five miles? Besides, I think it's lovely out here."

"Are you applying for the job?"

Jenny was surprised by Luke's offer. But after seeing the glint in his eyes she knew it was more a dare than anything else. If she didn't already have a job, she might consider taking him up on it. She wouldn't mind at all being with Garrett and Crissy.

"Maybe you should think about getting married," she countered.

He sobered quickly. "I've been there, and I'd rather not relive the experience, thank you."

Jenny wanted to ask a hundred question about Luke's marriage, but she knew if she did he would probably toss her out in the snow. "My brother Tyler had a bad first marriage, and he didn't want to chance getting hurt again. Until Maggie Carson came into his life." Jenny grinned. "They've been happily married for the last five years and have two kids."

Luke glared at her. "Good for him," he said sarcastically.

It was definitely time to change the subject, Jenny realized. But she doubted they could talk about anything without fighting. "How did the calves do in the storm?" she finally asked.

He wiped a hand over his face. "It's likely I've lost a few."

"I'm sorry, Luke." She truly was. She knew how hard ranching was and losing cattle was like losing a paycheck.

He shrugged. "If you're going to live in this part of the country, you have to get used to it. Or you don't survive."

"Great going, brother. You keep talking like this, you'll scare Ms. Murdock off."

Jenny turned and saw a tall, good-looking man about thirty. He had wavy auburn hair and sparkling blue eyes, and a smile that was sensual and flirty. She glanced back at Luke just in time to see his jaw tense.

"Hi, I'm Drew Reilly," he said as he crossed the room. "Happy to finally meet you, Ms. Murdock." He offered her his hand and she took it. "I'm so sorry that you were greeted by a storm on your first day in Last Hope."

"I'm glad to meet you, too. And please, call me Jenny," she said, somewhat relieved she was going to be leaving. "Since you made it here, the roads must be cleared," she said. "Did you find my car?"

The younger Reilly nodded. "Yes, but we can't get it out yet. The snow is pretty high out there," he explained. "We'll have to wait until tomorrow."

"Well, how am I going to get around without a car?"

Drew's smile reminded her of Luke. "Don't you worry about a thing. I'll drive you into town and get you settled in at the motel."

"But I don't have any clothes. My suitcases are in the trunk of my car."

"Do you have your keys?" he asked.

Jenny shook her head, embarrassed. "No, I dropped them in the snow when I tried to open the trunk."

He flashed her a smile again. "Don't you worry, we'll find the keys, or we'll have the locksmith make you a new set."

"You've got all the bases covered, huh, brother?" Luke said.

Drew's gaze remained on Jenny. "Just trying to make the lady comfortable, and allow her to sample a little of Last Hope's hospitality."

Luke mumbled something as Crissy and Garrett came into the room. Jenny was surprised that they weren't more excited to see their uncle. Instead, they went and stood next to their father.

"Jenny, are you going away?" Garrett asked.

"Just into town." She bent down. "You can come and visit me after I get settled. How would you like that?"

The boy nodded, and after a moment so did his sister. "Will you come back and see us?" he asked.

Jenny glanced up at Luke. "If it's all right with your father, sure I'd like to come for a visit."

Luke's expression remained impassive. "I told you you were welcome to ride anytime."

Jenny hugged both kids. "See, I'll be back, and we'll all go riding." She stood up and directed her attention to Luke. "Thanks for all your help. I don't know what I would have done if you hadn't come along."

Luke's eyes avoided her. "Just remember to dress warm and listen to the weather advisories."

"I will," she promised. Seeing the forlorn look on Crissy's and Garrett's faces, suddenly she didn't want to leave them.

Drew stepped forward. "Well, if we want to get into town before dark, we'd better get going. And while we're driving in, I'm going to do my darnedest to try to convince you to accept the job. I'll take you by the courthouse. The building is practically a historic monument, but there's a little money in the budget to decorate your office."

"What are you talking about?" Luke asked. "What office are you redecorating?"

Drew stopped at the door. "Well, Jenny's, of course. If I can talk her into it, she's going to be my new administrative assistant."

"You need an administrative assistant about as much as I do," he mumbled under his breath, but it was loud enough for his brother to hear.

"I'm the mayor of Last Hope." Drew grinned. "Brother, you should bring the kids into town more often and see some of the changes. Since I took office last January, we've drawn five new businesses into town. In another month, a Big D discount store will be breaking ground for their building on the south side and a meat-packing plant will be

moving to town. The downtown area is getting a face-lift."
He shook his head. "So many things going on, I need help."
He glanced at Jenny. "That's the reason I want you. I think
you would be terrific at the job and just the boost this town
needs."

Luke watched as Drew's compliments caused Jenny to
blush. He didn't like it, not one bit.

"I have a lot of plans for you, Jenny. I want you to head
a special project this summer. Oh, yes, Luke, Ms. Murdock is definitely going to be a great asset." He checked his
watch. "I think we better start back."

Luke stared at Jenny as his brother went out to his Jeep
and started it up. He shook his head. "You play your cards
right, Ms. Murdock, you may get more than a job. You may
just catch the most eligible man in town."

Jenny frowned. "What are you talking about?"

"You mean, my brother didn't tell you that he's looking
for a bride?"

Chapter Four

It took nearly two hours before Jenny arrived at the Cozy Country Inn. Drew had driven her to her car, and miraculously, they found her set of keys. But Mayor Reilly refused to allow her to drive into town, saying the roads were still too hazardous. Then he instructed a tow-truck driver to deliver her Ford Mustang to the motel.

Jenny had started to protest, but her common sense told her she hadn't had much experience driving in snow. She also realized that if she planned to stay in Wyoming, her little red car wouldn't be a practical vehicle. Whoa. Was she jumping the gun? Before making any decision, she wanted to know more about her job and see more of Last Hope. And Drew Reilly had offered to give her the guided tour.

Once settled in her room, Jenny opened her suitcase and took out a bra and pair of panties, thinking she was never again going to take clean underwear for granted. She walked into the bathroom, and her thoughts turned to the man she had spent the past twenty-hours with. Luke Reilly. He'd sure seemed happy to be finally getting rid of her, she thought with a pang a sadness.

She kicked off her shoes and unfastened her jeans, sliding them down her legs. The last thing she wanted to worry about was whether or not a cowboy with a bad attitude liked her, especially when a good-looking, agreeable man like Drew showed more than just a passing interest in her. She reached into the shower stall and turned on the water. After undressing, she stepped into the tub. Jenny closed her eyes, letting the warm spray wash over her body.

No two brothers could be less alike, she thought. Drew was outgoing and charming, and Luke seemed to be angry with the world. At least, he seemed to be angry with her. He'd let her know he didn't like her being in his house, and certainly hadn't been happy to know she might be settling in his town. Well, she had a right to have a life, to find happiness. And if Last Hope, Wyoming, made her happy, then she was going to stay. Besides, how often would she see the man if she lived in town and he lived on the ranch?

Jenny turned off the water and reached for a towel. "The Double R Ranch is thirty miles away," she murmured as she dried off. How often would they run into each other?

She wrapped the towel around her hair turban-style. After dressing in a pair of pleated navy slacks and an off-white blouse, she applied a little makeup, then blow-dried her hair into soft waves around her face. Then she hurried back into the bedroom and slipped on her loafers and checked her watch. She was running late and Drew was picking her up for dinner for more discussion about the job. Jenny was excited but nervous about the evening.

She'd had several jobs during her college years, everything from being a waitress and short-order cook to working as a gofer for Murdock Oil. Her biggest concern was whether she could handle the job and fit in here in Last Hope. Her thoughts went to Luke again.

Jenny sat down on the bed. She hadn't come all this way to let another man dictate to her. She'd had a lifetime of bossy males with bad tempers. And just because Luke had a great pair of shoulders and gorgeous brown eyes and kissed like a dream didn't mean he was potential husband material.

"What a shame," she breathed. Then she thought of Crissy and Garrett, realizing how quickly she'd gotten attached to them. One thing she could say for Luke, he was a good father. A warm feeling spread through her as she remembered the genuine love he showed for his family. He had also turned as ornery as a wounded bear when she'd accused him of not taking care of his children.

She shook her head. There was so much about Luke Reilly that confused her. From the time he'd found her stranded in the snow, his reassuring voice let her know she was safe. It was the same feeling when he'd lifted her into his strong arms and carried her into his home as if she were a priceless package. Her skin tingled, still able to feel his tender touch when he'd pulled her into his arms and kissed her. Never had she experienced such passion with a man. The sad part was, she knew he didn't trust her. Was it all women or just her?

Jenny drew a long breath and released it. Oh, what she wouldn't give to find out about the hurt he tried so hard to hide behind his eyes.

The knock on the door quickly brought her out of her reverie. *Pull yourself together, girl, and forget the cowboy. There's probably a town full of eligible men who wouldn't mind spending time with you.* She answered the door and was greeted by Drew, whose smile grew wider as his gaze combed over her.

"Wow, you look lovely," he said eagerly.

"Thank you," she answered, enjoying the view of the handsome mayor in a pair of khaki slacks, blue shirt and burgundy sweater.

"I hope you're hungry."

"Actually, I am."

"Good. There's a great steak house not far from here. But I thought first we'd take a run through town before it gets dark."

"I'd like that," Jenny said, her excitement renewed. She grabbed her purse and coat and went out the door. All thoughts of Luke disappeared as Drew helped her into his Jeep.

Jenny followed the waitress across the bloodred carpet to the booth in Charlie's Steak House. The walls were paneled in dark wood and wagon-wheel chandeliers hung overhead. A familiar country-western ballad played softly over the conversations in the half-filled restaurant. Drew sat down across from her and glanced up at the young woman asking for their drink order.

"I'll have iced tea," Jenny said.

"The same for me," he agreed.

Once the waitress left, he spoke. "I know it doesn't look very fancy, but I'll guarantee they cook up the best steak and ribs around."

"You better be careful about that claim, Mayor. Remember, I'm a Texas girl. We're pretty partial to our own home-grown beef."

He smiled once again and leaned back. "I'm not worried. I'm more concerned about talking you into accepting my job offer and staying."

Jenny grew serious as he tried to tempt her further with a generous salary and medical benefits. "The other perk is that I'm only a part-time mayor, so you won't have me breathing down your neck every minute. You'd pretty much be on your own. And I'm open to any suggestions and new ideas that will help this town."

Earlier during their drive through the small community of four thousand, Drew had explained more about his ideas for Last Hope.

The waitress appeared with their drinks and set them on the table, then took their orders. After she left, Drew continued, "One of my campaign promises was to bring economic growth to Last Hope, and for the coal miners, to entice more women to this area." He grinned. "Am I enticing you?"

"Could be," Jenny answered.

"Well, if you decide to take the job as my administrative assistant, your duties will be to help with correspondence, answer the phones and arrange my schedule. There will be a few social functions I'll have to attend...." He raised an eyebrow in question. "Would you have any problem going with me? I mean...it would be nice to take you...as my assistant, of course." He raised a hand and quickly added, "But that doesn't mean you *have* to go."

Jenny smiled. "Drew, when we talked over the phone, I told you that if I accept this job, I'm eager to help you in any way I can."

"Of course, most of the social functions I'm talking about are held at the local churches." Drew smiled once again. "But they'll probably draw the best attendance in years with you there."

"Why is that?" Jenny asked.

"Well, for one thing, you're the prettiest woman we've had here since the country-fair queen visited two summers ago."

She was taken aback with his flirting. "Thank you."

"I hope I'm not acting like a fool." He sighed as he leaned back in the booth. "I just want this interview to go well."

"It is going well." Jenny was definitely intrigued with the town of Last Hope, and its handsome Mayor. "I just have a lot to think about," she added. "For one thing, I'd be moving away from my family."

Drew gave her a sober look. "I understand how difficult that can be. But Last Hope is a nice community, and you'll make a lot of friends here."

And no one here has ever heard of the Murdocks, Jenny added silently.

Jenny's thoughts were interrupted when the weathered doors of the restaurant opened and two men walked in. Her hand tightened around her glass when she noticed the tall, dark-haired man was none other than Luke Reilly. He was dressed in black jeans, a white shirt practically covered by a sheepskin coat, and his boots looked new. She glanced up as he pulled off his hat, and she saw his freshly shaven face and neatly combed hair. What was he doing here? she wondered, hoping he wouldn't notice her. She'd had enough of Mr. Reilly to last a long time.

At that moment, he turned toward her and his smile disappeared. A glare replaced it as he glanced at her dinner companion. Luke spoke to the older gentleman with him, then started for her table.

Feeling like a trapped animal, Jenny could only watch as he approached.

"Well, well, Ms. Murdock," Luke began. "Doesn't look like you're wasting any time." He turned to his brother.

Drew didn't hide his displeasure. "Look, Luke, if you don't mind, Jenny and I are discussing business."

"Oh, working after hours, are we?"

"If that's what it takes to get Jenny to decide to stay in Last Hope."

Luke's gaze returned to Jenny. "What more do you want, Jenny? Or do you want him to beg?"

An angry Drew opened his mouth to speak when the waitress came by the table to inform him he had an important phone call. Drew stood. "Excuse me, Jenny. I'll only be a minute." He glanced at his brother. "Behave, or you'll have to answer to me."

The last thing Jenny wanted was to be alone with Luke, but she tried to act pleasant. "What brings you to town?" She looked around. "Where are Crissy and Garrett?"

Luke slid into the seat across from her and leaned back, making himself comfortable. "Don't worry, Ms. Murdock, I have a few friends that are willing to come to my rescue when I have to conduct business."

Jenny cocked an eyebrow as she saw Luke's dinner guest go into the bar. "Well, everyone needs friends."

"Has my brother seduced you into taking the job as his assistant?"

Jenny stiffened. "There is no seduction involved. This is a business arrangement."

Luke's smile was more of a smirk. "Hang around a while and give my brother a little time."

"Look, I don't know what you have against me. Maybe you just don't like me. I can handle that." No, she couldn't. "But at least give me a chance at this job."

"I don't have a problem with the job." Luke grew serious. "It's the manhunt that bothers me."

Jenny clenched her fists and fought to stay calm. "The only thing I'm on is a job interview, Mr. Reilly. So, if you'll excuse me..."

Luke sat there for a moment longer. What was it about this woman that got him so riled? So what if his brother had his sights set on her. Drew had dated lots of women. Luke hadn't. And Cindy had left enough scars to last him a lifetime. "Don't pretend you aren't on the prowl for a husband." Luke got up when he saw his brother across the room.

"Who do you think you are?" she began, her dark eyes lit with fire, "telling me what I can and can't do. The last I heard, this was a free country, Wyoming included."

Drew slid into the booth. "Sorry about the interruption," the mayor apologized.

Jenny forced a smile. "No problem. It just gave me time to think over your offer. I've decided to accept."

Drew grinned. "That's great. What made you decide?"

She glanced at Luke. "Oh, I'd say you owe a great deal to your brother. He more or less talked me into it."

Jenny watched as Luke tensed. Served him right for nosing into her business.

"This calls for a celebration," Drew said. "Luke, since you were the one to convince Jenny to stay, why don't you join us?"

"No, I can't. I have business of my own." He glared at his brother. "Ranch business. I'm having dinner with Clint Weeks to discuss loaning out two of our breeding bulls. Maybe you should sit in on this one, too."

Drew waved his hand in the air. "You can handle the cattle. Of course, if you're ready to talk about the mineral rights, I'll be more than willing to listen."

With a mumbled curse, Luke turned and stormed off.

Jenny was beginning to see there was more than just a physical difference between the Reilly brothers.

Three days later, Jenny walked up the steps of the old brick courthouse. The stately building with its weathered pillars had stood for nearly eighty years, and showed signs of needing a face-lift. The roof leaked, the paint was peeling around the windows and the fountain in the courtyard hadn't worked in thirty years.

These were just some of the things Drew had wanted repaired along with the completion of the downtown renovation. After one day of trying to keep up with the young, enthusiastic Mayor Reilly, Jenny was convinced he would get everything done by the Fourth of July celebration. The man had way too much energy for his own good. That night, Jenny had gone back to her motel room and fallen into bed from exhaustion.

Today, things were different. After a good night's sleep, Jenny was up at six. Excited about her first day on the job, she dressed three different times before deciding to wear a navy business suit. Too nervous to eat any breakfast, she drove into town and parked outside the courthouse. It was only seven-thirty, but she was anxious to get an early start.

The front door was already unlocked. It was probably maintenance, Jenny thought, remembering having met the janitor, Fred Cox, the day before. Fred was about thirty-five and only a few inches taller than herself. He had a friendly smile and told her that if she ever needed anything, just to call down to the basement.

Jenny started down the marble-tiled hall, her heels tapping out a staccato cadence in the empty corridor as she passed the city council chambers, then the mayor's office. Farther down was her new workplace. She unlocked the door and went inside, inhaling the faint odor of paint. Sandalwood was the color someone had chosen for her office. It was furnished with a desk, almost too big for the room, along with two file cabinets and a bookcase. She went to the window that overlooked the town square.

Jenny took a deep breath and surveyed the view of her new home. It was a charming scene. Last week's snow had all but disappeared, and the trees and shrubs along Main Street were starting to bloom. The stone and brick buildings in the square had freshly painted trim and new awnings. Jenny looked at the restaurant on the corner, Molly's Kitchen, which seemed to be the most popular place in town. She watched as several customers moved in and out through the bright red doors.

Maybe it was time she started her morning, too. Jenny turned around to her desk. Although it was bare, she knew she had more than enough to keep her busy. She pulled out her chair. Where to begin? she wondered.

Suddenly, there was a knock on her door and a woman peeked inside. It was Ruth Foster, the attractive, middle-aged blonde who was the town clerk.

"You're here bright and early," Ruth said. "It's too bad you aren't getting paid by the hour." She walked inside carrying two steaming coffee mugs and a bag of doughnuts that smelled heavenly. "Thought I might try to bribe the new help."

Jenny blinked. "I was told to be nice to you so I'll get my paycheck on time." Smiling, she accepted the mug from Ruth.

"Hey, I'm just happy to have you here. Ever since Emily
Meehan retired, I've been doing all the mayor's correspondence." The woman sat on the edge of the desk and reached
for a jelly doughnut, then motioned for Jenny to take one.
"They're from Molly's. I swear, they're the best you'll ever
eat. My hips are proof of that." The woman glanced down
at her snug skirt. "If you don't have plans for lunch today,
we can run by there and I'll introduce you to Molly Willis.
She makes the most delicious..." Her voice trailed off and
Ruth looked thoughtful for a minute, then said, "I can't
remember anything I don't like that Molly cooks."

They both laughed and Jenny bit into a doughnut, and
felt herself beginning to relax. "Oh, these *are* good." No
wonder all those people were at the restaurant, Jenny
thought as she opened her mouth to take another bite. When
she heard loud voices outside her office, she looked at Ruth
questioningly.

"Must be Drew and his brother." The clerk took another
drink from her mug, as if she wasn't even curious. As the
sound grew louder, Jenny set down her doughnut and went
to the door. She looked into the hall, where Luke and Drew
were involved in a heated discussion. So, the other night
wasn't a fluke. They really didn't get along.

Their disagreeing didn't bother her as much as the fact
that Garrett was standing alongside his father. Just then, the
boy turned around and his eyes lit up when he saw her.

"Jenny, Jenny," he cried as he ran into her arms, nearly
knocking her over as he hugged her. "You're here." He
looked up at her. "Crissy said you moved away, 'cause you
didn't come back." He shook his head and grinned. "But I
knew you'd stay."

Jenny felt bad. Although she'd only been in town less
than a week, she should have called the kids. She knelt
down. "I'm sorry, Garrett, I've been so busy with finding
a place to live and with my new job that I—" She stopped.
This child didn't need to hear her excuses. "Will you forgive me?"

Garrett nodded. "Will you come and see me?"

"Sure, as soon as I get settled in an apartment." She stood up and took the boy's hand, noticing that Drew and Luke were both watching her. "How about if I take Garrett into my office while you two discuss your... business?"

Luke studied her for a moment, then nodded. Drew unlocked his office. "Maybe it would be better if we take this inside," the younger brother suggested. Reluctantly, Luke followed him through the door.

"C'mon, Garrett. You can see my new office."

"Okay," he agreed.

Inside, Jenny lifted him up onto her desk. "Garrett, this is Ruth."

"Howdy, Garrett," Ruth said, shaking his hand. "We met last spring when your daddy came in to pay his taxes. But I bet you don't remember me."

"Sure," the boy said. "You got a big jar of peppermint candies on your desk."

Both women laughed. "Now you see how I entice the men in this town," the older woman said.

"Hey, if it works, go for it," Jenny advised and offered Garrett a doughnut from the bag. She eyed the attractive woman who looked to be about fifty-five, then glanced down at her ringless finger. "Are you looking for someone special?"

"You mean, a man?" Ruth shrugged. "My husband died a few years back. And with my kids grown and gone, I wouldn't mind passing time with a nice gentleman."

"Wouldn't we all," Jenny answered, wiping a smudge of sugar glaze off Garrett's chin. "I think I'll just wait until this guy grows up."

"I think a better idea might be to take a shot at his daddy."

Jenny gave her an incredulous look. "You've got to be kidding. I've been in this town less than a week, and Luke Reilly acts like I'm carrying the plague."

"My daddy thinks you're pretty," Garrett said as he chewed his doughnut. "He told me."

The two women exchanged glances. Ruth was the first to speak. "See, you should go after him." She lowered her voice. "And you get this cute little guy in the package, too."

"Ruth, you haven't been listening," Jenny whispered back. "Luke Reilly wants nothing to do with me."

Ruth waved her hand in the air. "I've known both the Reillys since they were boys. Luke has always been a little too serious, but he's a good man. He just speaks his mind."

"I know. And he's more or less told me that he doesn't like me."

"I never said that," a familiar voice rang out.

Luke was standing in the doorway.

Jenny felt the heat rise to her cheeks as a huge lump swelled in her throat. Unable to speak, she glanced at Ruth for help.

The older woman ignored her, giving her attention to Garrett. "Oh, my, what a mess you are, young man. How 'bout we go and get you cleaned up before you leave little fingerprints all over Jenny's new office?" Garrett didn't protest as Ruth helped him off the desk and strolled to the door. Luke stepped aside to let them through. Then, not taking his eyes off Jenny, he ambled inside, his intimidating size quickly filling up the space in the small office.

"Believe me, Ms. Murdock, if I disliked you, you would have been left to fend for yourself during the blizzard."

Jenny fought to keep from retreating behind her desk. She squared her shoulders, trying to tell herself that Luke Reilly was no different than Ty and Brett. And she wasn't going to let this man bully her, either. "It isn't your nature to leave people or animals stranded, Mr. Reilly. It's just that women aren't at the top of your list." She watched his jaw flinch and knew she'd hit a nerve. What woman had caused the flash of pain she saw in his dark eyes?

"That might be because they turn on you so easily."

She found herself wishing she could change his thinking. "Maybe it could be the way you handle them."

He took a step closer. "How would you suggest I handle a woman?"

Jenny felt his breath against her face and a warm shiver raced down her spine. She raised her eyes to his and was instantly drawn into their smoldering raven depths. She nervously cleared her throat and somehow found her voice. "With respect. Treat us as equals. We have a lot to contribute besides waiting on a man and having babies."

Slowly, a smile spread across Luke's face. "Is that the reason you came all the way to Last Hope, to find... respect?"

"One of the reasons." Her brothers came to mind, and Jenny wondered what they were doing with all their free time, now that they didn't have her to watch over.

"And if you happen to find a husband?"

Jenny's patience finally ran out. "What is your problem? Are you afraid that I'm going to catch some poor, unsuspecting man and trick him into marrying me?" she asked. "And when he's not looking, steal his money and run off?"

Luke couldn't help staring at Jenny Murdock. Not only was she pretty, but a feisty little thing. He would bet she could kick and bite with the best of them. Of course, that wasn't the first thing that came to mind as his gaze traveled over her shapely body. "It happens...."

"And it can happen the other way around, too."

Luke caught the flash of sadness in her eyes before she glanced away and walked to her desk. He wondered if a man had been the one who caused it.

Before he had a chance to ask, Garrett came running into the room, all traces of doughnut cleaned off his face. "Ruth showed me how to use her computer. Dad, can I stay here while you go to work? You can pick me up when Crissy gets out of school."

Luke knew this might happen coming to the courthouse. Jenny Murdock had been all Garrett talked about this past week, and running into her today wasn't what he needed. "I'm sorry, son, you can't today." Luke watched as his son stared down at the toy figures in his hand. "Maybe another time."

"Maybe after I get settled in," Jenny added. "When you come by to see your Uncle Drew, you can visit with me, too." She knelt beside the child. "I'll have more doughnuts."

"But we never come to see Uncle Drew."

Luke reached for his son's hand, not wanting to air any more of the family's private business. "C'mon, Garrett, we better get going. I have to check the herd."

Garrett pulled from his father's grasp and hugged Jenny goodbye. "Will you come back to the ranch someday?"

Jenny wasn't sure what to do. She looked up at Luke in time to see his nod. "Sure, I'll come by and see you and Crissy as soon as I can get away."

"Okay." He took his father's hand again and together they walked out the door.

Ruth appeared seconds later. "So, how did it go?"

"How did what go?" Jenny asked innocently.

"C'mon, I left you two alone hoping you could get something started."

Jenny dropped into her chair and leaned back. "Well, I was wrong, Ruth. Luke doesn't dislike me." She glanced up at the town clerk's hopeful look. "He dislikes all women."

Chapter Five

A little over a week later, Jenny walked into her apartment and closed the door. She tossed her purse on the table and immediately kicked off her shoes. With a sigh, she curled her stocking feet into the plush carpet, then went to the sofa and sat down. As tired as she felt, she couldn't hide her smile when she looked around the small living room. This all belonged to her.

There was a secondhand, sample-stitch print love seat and a scratched coffee table, which she was going to refinish as soon as she found time. The two end tables were in a little better shape, but they were going to be redone, too. Her kitchen still looked bare, but thanks to Ruth Foster, she at least had dishes and a set of cookware. Not only had the town clerk given her things to help furnish her apartment, she also went with her to shop at the local thrift stores. All but her queen-size bed was bought secondhand, but Jenny loved the potential antiques she had picked out over the weekend. Now all she needed was a few personal things, like pictures for the walls, some family photos, and this place would be just like home.

There was a soft knock on the door and Jenny went to answer it. She was greeted by a small, blond woman about her age and height. Dressed in a pair of jeans and a bright pink blouse, she held a plate of home-baked cookies.

"Hi, I'm Shelly Hart. I live in 107." She smiled. "I thought I'd stop by and say welcome to the neighborhood. But if you're busy, I can come back."

"No, please, come in," Jenny said as she stepped aside. "I'm Jenny Murdock."

"I know. I asked Mrs. Crawley, the landlady," Shelly offered. "She also told me you just moved here from Texas. I came four months ago from Kansas."

"Really? How do you like it here so far?" Jenny directed Shelly to the sofa and offered her a seat.

"My job is great. I'm a fifth-grade teacher at the Hope School. And the people are nice. But socially, there isn't a lot to offer."

"Well, it's a small town," Jenny said, remembering how back home she and her friends used to have to drive into Denton for any nightlife. "I've only been here a couple of weeks and I'm so busy learning my job, I guess I haven't paid attention."

"You're working for Mayor Reilly, aren't you?"

"I'm supposed to be his administrative assistant, but so far all I've been doing is filing and meeting people."

Shelly grinned. "They're just excited to see a newcomer and want to be friendly. How many men have asked you out so far?"

Jenny didn't hide her surprise. "None. Why?"

"Because there are a lot more men here than women."

Jenny sat down in the folding chair next to the sofa. "Maybe, uh, you better explain."

"It seems the town's population has been declining the past few years. They took a local census a while back, and they discovered that there are three times the number of men to women."

"My, that's a lot."

"There are several coal mines in this area and a lot of ranches. And more and more kids are going away to college and not returning." Shelly waved her hand in the air. "Anyway, when Mayor Reilly was campaigning, he promised he would promote economic growth in Last Hope. But the single men in town suggested he promote some social growth, too. Drew Reilly said he'd do what he could. Did you come here looking for a husband?"

"Not exactly," Jenny answered, not wanting to go into detail about her past. "I left Texas to get out on my own. Away from an overprotective family."

"I'm not exactly advertising it, but I moved here hoping to find a husband. I got tired of the men in Kansas City wanting everything but marriage." The pretty blonde raised an eyebrow. "If you know what I mean."

Jenny nodded as she thought back to the phone conversation with Drew Reilly and his curiosity about her marital status. And if her family would mind her relocating in Wyoming.

"I guess I'm a little old-fashioned," Shelly continued, "but I'm holding out for marriage."

"And my brothers made sure I did, too," Jenny murmured to herself.

"You're lucky to have a job working for the mayor. He's very handsome."

"He is that," Jenny agreed. Too bad she couldn't get intrigued by Drew. As much as she hated to admit it, her mind kept wandering to Luke Reilly.

Jenny offered her neighbor a soft drink, and for the next thirty minutes they spent getting to know each other while munching on homemade cookies. Then Jenny showed Shelly around her apartment. They were just coming out of the bedroom, when there was another knock on the door.

Excited about having two guests in one night, Jenny rushed to answer it. She didn't expect to find Luke Reilly standing on the other side.

"Luke," she said breathlessly. He had on new-looking jeans and a slightly wrinkled Western shirt, but it didn't take away from his broad shoulders and muscular chest. He pulled off his tan Stetson and strands of black hair fell across his forehead. Jenny had to put her hand behind her back to keep from reaching out and brushing it away.

"Were you expecting someone else?"

"Oh, no. Come in."

Luke looked cautious as he stepped across the threshold and glanced around the room. "Looks like you're getting settled."

"Yes, I bought furniture this weekend," Jenny stated proudly. "Drew helped me move in."

"No doubt."

She didn't miss the sarcasm in his tone, but luckily didn't have to continue the conversation because just then Shelly came out of the bedroom. Jenny introduced the two, then her neighbor excused herself and headed for the door. She tried to talk Shelly into staying, but to no avail. When Jenny returned to the living room, she found Luke still standing, holding on to his hat. Why was he here?

"I know you didn't come by to welcome me to Last Hope." She wasn't going to give him a chance to start anything. "Is there something I can do for you?"

He reached inside his shirt pocket and pulled out one of her barrettes. "I found this in my bedroom." His voice was husky, making it sound as if they'd had an intimate weekend together.

"Thanks." Jenny reached for it and their hands brushed. She felt a tingle up her arm and quickly pulled back. "I was wondering where this was," she lied, knowing she had many just like it.

"As far as I'm concerned," he told her, "you can throw it away. You should wear your hair down."

Jenny swallowed. "Oh, really?"

Luke felt like a fool, and crazy, to boot, for coming to Jenny's apartment. Just leave her be, he had told himself at least a hundred times in the past week. But he couldn't seem to stay away from her. "Really."

Her eyes met his, and for a moment she studied him intently. "Why are you saying this, Luke?"

He stepped closer. "Hell if I know." He reached out and brushed her long chestnut hair away from her face. She looked so feminine dressed in her short skirt and ruffled blouse. He liked the fact that he could see her gorgeous legs...and bare feet. Only two weeks ago, those cute painted toes had been sticking out from under his big bathrobe.

"I guess I like to live dangerously," he said as he tipped her head back. "I bet you like a little danger, too."

The only answer was the husky sound of her whispering his name. His body stirred painfully.

God! She had to be the sweetest thing he'd ever laid eyes on. He started to lower his head when reality hit him. He didn't need the complications of a woman in his life, no matter how much he wanted her.

Luke drew back slightly, feeling the erratic pounding of his heart. "Ah, Jenny, you are dangerous," he said and released her. "Too dangerous for me." He started for the door.

Jenny blinked several times before she came out of her trance. "Wait..." She caught up with Luke. "You came all the way into town, to...to give me back a barrette that isn't worth two dollars?"

She watched, fascinated, as his eyes warmed.

"Yeah, and Garrett wanted me to invite you to come out to the ranch. We thought, since the weather's been nice, you'd like to go riding."

Jenny opened her mouth to tell him that she didn't want anything to do with him, but something kept her from saying it. Maybe it was the fact that he wanted to kiss her as much as she wanted to kiss him. But she wouldn't give him the satisfaction of letting him think he could get whatever he wanted...easily.

She folded her arms across her chest. "I'll think about it."

* * *

Jenny marched into the courthouse the next day, her determined stride taking her straight to the mayor's office. She knocked on the door, then without waiting for an invitation, she walked in. She found Drew on the phone and he waved for her to have a seat. Jenny went to the window instead and looked down into the town square.

Surprisingly, there was a lot of activity; preschool-age children were playing in the small park, mothers keeping a watch from a nearby bench. Gardeners were busy trimming the trees and shrubs. They were even adding colorful bedding plants around the courthouse fountain. Of course, it was spring, Jenny thought as she glanced up at the sunny blue sky. But it had been only two weeks since the blizzard.

Drew hung up the phone and came to the window. "What can I do for you?"

"I have a question." Jenny leaned against the window ledge. "Did you hire me because you thought I could do the job, or because I'm a single woman?"

Drew couldn't hide the flush that spread across his cheeks. "I hired you because you were the best for the job."

Jenny sighed. "What job, Drew? All I've done so far is file and answer the phone. My great-aunt Alma could do that."

He raised his hand. "You'll do more. I just wanted to make sure you were settled in. Believe me, Jenny, I need you."

For what? she wondered. "All right. If I'm to be your assistant, why didn't you tell me about the census? And the fact that there are nearly three men to every woman?" She began to pace the room. "At least now I understand why I've held such fascination to the people in this town. They see me as a potential bride."

"I'm sorry, Jenny." He looked truly embarrassed. "I should have explained things. Believe me, I didn't bring you here as a mail-order bride. But over the last few years, we haven't had many new residents, male or female, in Last Hope."

"There's Shelly Hart, the new teacher at the school."

Drew frowned. "I guess I did meet her."

"Well, she's single and available. But from what she told me last night, this town doesn't offer much of a social life."

"The church does a social every year," Drew said. "But the women who show up are with their husbands. There just aren't enough women to go around." He gave her a pained expression. "Believe me, I know. I've been looking myself. The young women around here leave town to go to large cities."

"Then do something to bring them back here."

"I've been working on it. As you know, I've already got several small businesses to locate in Last Hope. And with the discount store and the meat-packing plant, there will be more jobs for the community."

"But you need to concentrate on a little social growth, too."

"I want to, but I don't know how to get things started."

"Maybe a little organized matchmaking would help. You need to sponsor some get-togethers. Make it attractive for women to stick around. Make people realize that Last Hope is a nice community in which to settle down and raise a family." All at once, Jenny's head was going crazy with ideas. "A small town in Minnesota made a plea on television, looking for people to move there, offering—especially women—business opportunities."

Drew gave her an incredulous look. "You want me to go on TV?"

Jenny bit back a smile. "First, let's start with a few social events here and see how things go."

"Sounds great. You can be in charge."

"Wait," she protested. "Where do I start?"

"I don't know. Maybe talk to Pastor Wilson over at the First Calvary Church," Drew said as he began to gather papers off his desk and put them in his briefcase. "They have a nice big hall." He started for the door. "I'll be out all morning and afternoon with meetings. Page me if you need anything." He checked his watch. "How 'bout I buy you lunch at Molly's around one o'clock and we'll go over what you've come up with?"

Jenny was busy taking notes as Drew walked to the door. "Use my Rolodex for any phone numbers you might need," he called over his shoulder. Suddenly, he stopped and grinned. "I knew you'd be perfect for the job." Then he was gone.

Jenny also smiled. "Finally, something I can get into."

Later that day, Luke was sitting at the counter in Molly's Kitchen, finishing a second cup of coffee. Garrett was busy polishing off his hamburger and fries. After the morning's routine of feeding the stock and checking his herd, he'd been a little restless.

So he'd told his son they were coming into town for lunch. He hadn't visited with Tom and Molly in a while, so he could catch up on all the news. And there was no better place to do that than at Molly's Kitchen.

Luke glanced in the mirror behind the counter and froze as he saw Jenny Murdock come through the door. There was the reason for his spring fever. She stood for a minute as if she was looking for someone. Her hair was pulled back, leaving some dark curls dancing off her delicate shoulders, which caused her brown eyes to look even larger. Dressed in a red dress with a wide belt that showed off her small waist, she was sexy enough to get a man thinking about things he had no business thinking. Like how badly he'd wanted to kiss her last night.

"Now that's the prettiest thing I've seen around these parts since Molly came to visit her aunt Mae nearly forty years ago," Tom Willis said from the next stool. "Is that the new gal Drew hired?"

Luke nodded.

Tom gave him a curious look. "You rescued that beauty and handed her over to your brother?"

Tom Willis had been sheriff for as long as Luke could remember. Now, at nearly sixty, and a few pounds overweight and slightly balding, he was still the most respected man in the county. And Luke's best friend.

"I didn't hand her over to anyone." Luke's gaze followed her as Jenny found an empty booth. "She went of her own free will."

"Most women do, when a man doesn't extend an invitation to stay," Molly said as she added coffee to both Luke's and her husband's cups.

Luke studied the tall, slender woman behind the counter. At fifty-five, she had short gray hair and wore it curled around her face. Even with the laugh lines around her eyes and mouth, she was a pretty woman. And Molly and Tom Willis were crazy about each other.

"I don't extend invitations to women anymore."

"Maybe that's the reason you're so grumpy all the time," Molly teased. And despite himself, Luke joined in the laughter.

"C'mon, you go over there and keep that poor girl company, before one of these other yahoos starts giving her a bad time."

"Believe me, she doesn't need any protection." *Only from me,* Luke thought.

"Can you take me over and introduce me to Jenny, Garrett?" Molly asked. "She came into the restaurant last week, but I wasn't here."

The boy's eyes lit up as he swung around and spotted Jenny. He couldn't climb off the stool fast enough and hurried to the booth. Luke watched as his lucky son received a big hug and invitation to sit down. Then Molly appeared at the booth and sat across the table from Jenny. The women exchanged a handshake and began to talk.

"Oh, no, you're in trouble now," Tom said. "Molly's probably telling her your life story."

Luke made a snorting sound. "I don't have many secrets left." Everyone in town had known about Cindy's affairs, he just happened to be the last one to find out.

Tom swung around on his stool. "I know I've given you a lot of advice over the years. I hope some of it has done you a little good. But you can't let what Cindy did ruin the rest of your life. Those kids of yours are too young to go without a mother. And your disposition would improve a whole helluva lot if you found yourself a good woman." He tugged on Luke's arm. "C'mon, introduce me to the pretty lady."

Luke stood up and strolled down the aisle toward the booth. This was not a good idea, he thought. He was already attracted to the woman, and he didn't need to push it any further. But by the looks of things, his kid and friends were doing that for him.

"Dad, Jenny said she can come to the ranch on Sunday." Garrett's eyes sparkled. "Right after she goes to church. Can we go to church, too? Huh, Dad, can we?"

"We'll talk about it later, son." Luke's gaze went to Jenny's tempting mouth, and he felt an unwelcome surge of excitement. "Jenny."

"Hi, Luke."

"This is Tom Willis. You can tell by the uniform, he's the sheriff around here. He's the one who radioed me about your car parked on the side of the road during the storm."

"Happy to meet you, Sheriff." Jenny offered her hand. "And finally be able to thank you for helping me out of the blizzard."

The older man grinned as his large hand nearly engulfed hers. "It's nice to meet you, too. As for the big rescue, I was just doin' my job. Besides, Luke here did all the work."

"And put up with an overnight guest, to boot," Jenny added.

"Bet Garrett liked having you sleep over," Molly said. "Didn't you, son?"

The five-year-old grinned. "Jenny's neat. She plays Go Fish, and she knows about Power Rangers."

Tom and Molly exchanged a knowing look. Luke knew this could only mean trouble.

Jenny ruffled the boy's hair. "I have young nephews back in Texas," she told Molly and Tom.

Luke tensed when he saw Drew come into the restaurant. His brother was dressed in a dark suit and a paisley tie. His light-colored hair was neatly trimmed and styled. He looked out of place in a blue-collar diner. Drew worked his way down the aisle, making polite conversation with some of the patrons before he arrived at their booth.

"What's going on?" Drew asked.

"We were just getting acquainted with the newest resident of Last Hope," Tom volunteered.

"Well, if you're telling her all the good points about Last Hope, I'm all for it," Drew teased. "I want to make sure I don't lose her."

Luke didn't like hearing his brother talk about Jenny in such personal terms. Just how personal was it between them? He straightened. Why should he care? "C'mon, Garrett, you have to finish your hamburger."

"But I want to talk to Jenny."

"You can talk to her Sunday."

The child slid out of the booth. "Don't forget."

"I won't," Jenny promised. She waved as Garrett, Molly and Tom walked back to the counter, leaving only Drew, Luke and herself.

Drew checked his watch. "Luke, we need to talk. Maybe you can come by my office later?"

"Maybe not," Luke interrupted. "I don't have time to keep running into town." He leaned closer to his brother. "But I'll tell you now, the answer is still no."

"Dammit, Luke," Drew said through his teeth. "You don't even know what I'm asking."

"I'll bet you a ten spot that it has a lot to do with mineral rights. And I think, bro, we're talked out on that subject." Luke turned back to Jenny. "See you Sunday."

Jenny could only stare into his dark compelling eyes and nod. He turned and walked away.

She was still following Luke's lazy gait, when Drew slid into the booth across from her.

"You can tell me to mind my own business," he began, "but if you're thinking about seeing my brother, there are things you should know."

She looked at the man across from her. "I'm only going out there because of Garrett's invitation," she lied. "There is nothing between Luke and me besides his letting me ride one of his horses."

Drew seemed relieved. "Good, I don't think Luke is the kind of man you should be seeing."

Jenny tensed, trying to hold off her rising anger. He was sounding too much like her brother Tyler. "Drew, maybe we should get something straight. I appreciate your concern, but I'm very capable of deciding who I go out with."

All she got from Drew was a nod, and the subject changed to business. "Did you get hold of Pastor Wilson?" he asked.

"Yes, and he suggested that I set up a meeting with the hospitality guild at the church. He told me to call Lucy Chance. Lucy and I talked about scheduling a meeting for next Monday afternoon." She looked up from her notebook. "What do you think?"

Drew leaned forward. "The important thing is what you think. Can you put a mixer together and find enough single women to come?"

Jenny wasn't sure what she could do. "If we advertise in surrounding towns, maybe hire a popular country western band and have door prizes..." She shrugged. "If it's successful, we can have another one. Maybe form a singles' club and have more activities through the summer, like picnics and hayrides. Make it something for all age groups, not just the young or senior citizens. And we can't forget the divorced and...widowed." Jenny caught the mayor staring at her. "What?"

"It just sounds like you've been working hard on this project," he said.

Thanks to Ruth, she'd had a busy day. "Ruth thought it would be a good idea if I went out to the Powder River Mining Company to talk with her brother. He's a foreman."

"What did you find out?"

"Well, Butch can't help me directly, but he promised he would pass out fliers for any social events we might have." She paused for a moment, then said, "We can also use local radio stations for advertising."

"That's a great idea." His hand reached across the table and rested on top of hers, squeezing gently. "Let's celebrate."

Jenny eased her hand away. "Whoa, it's a little too soon for that. Besides, all I did was make some phone calls."

"You came up with the ideas, and I know that you're going to follow through on them. Let me at least take you out to dinner tonight." Drew's blue eyes were glowing. He was a handsome man, and had a good future ahead of him. Someone her family would wholeheartedly approve of.

"Okay, we can go over a few more ideas I have," Jenny suggested, knowing she wanted to keep this relationship purely business. She glanced toward the counter where Luke was straddling a stool. One Reilly brother was all she could handle.

Chapter Six

Jenny drove her car along the gravel road leading to the Reilly ranch. The big two-story brick house came into view and took her breath away. Its white shutters gleamed in the sunlight, along with the new-looking shingles on the sloped roof. The trees and bushes surrounding the house were blooming with color, and off in the distance the majestic mountains made a perfect backdrop to the scenic picture.

She parked in front of the house and looked around. Where was everyone? She climbed out of the car and glanced toward the pasture and saw several horses grazing there. She drew a deep breath and started in the direction of the barn, wondering what kind of reception she would get from Luke. She never knew from one minute to the next how he would treat her.

Suddenly, Garrett came running from the house calling her name. Jenny had to swallow her laughter when he nearly tripped before he reached her.

"I've been looking for you all day," he managed to say between gulps of air.

"You were? But I wasn't supposed to be here until now. Did you get all your chores done?"

He nodded. "I helped Crissy with the dishes."

Jenny hugged him. "I'm proud of you."

The boy rewarded her with a big grin that reminded her of Luke.

"Where's your dad?"

"He's in the barn." Garrett took her hand. "C'mon, he's getting the horses saddled."

Jenny felt her excitement grow as she followed the boy into the barn. She hadn't been able to concentrate on work the past few days thinking about today, and seeing Luke.

The sun disappeared once she walked through the double doors. She stopped and glanced around the large structure. The building was old, but well-kept. The stalls were clean, and bales of hay were neatly stacked along the wall. She strolled past the tack room seeing it was just as organized, then continued to the last stall where she found Luke tending his pregnant mare.

"Hi," she said and climbed onto the bottom railing next to Garrett. "How's she doing?"

Luke gave her a quick glance as he stroked the animal. Jenny's gaze followed the action of his strong hands.

"She's doing fine. Still got another two weeks, though," Luke said as the mare shifted restlessly. "This is Sassy's first, and she's a little impatient."

Jenny reached out to the horse's muzzle. The animal nudged her hand right away. "Poor Sassy," she crooned as she stroked the animal.

"Dad said I can name her colt," Garrett volunteered.

"But it can't be a dumb name," Crissy called as she came toward the stall and climbed onto the railing. "Hi, Jenny."

"Hi, Crissy. How have you been?"

The girl rolled her eyes. "Bored, taking care of him."

"I take care of myself," Garrett said.

"Hey, if you two start fighting, you can spend the afternoon in your rooms," Luke said.

Both children immediately closed their mouths.

Luke came out of the stall and shut the gate. He had everyone follow him outside to the back of the barn, where three horses and a pony were saddled and tied to the fence.

Garrett ran up to the gray pony. "This is Willie."

"He's a beauty," Jenny said as she patted the docile animal.

"That's Crissy's horse, Calico." He pointed to the white mare with the red and black patches.

Luke stood back and watched Jenny as she examined the animals. He had no doubt she knew her way around a horse. She walked toward the brown roan mare he'd chosen for her to ride and stroked the animal gently.

"Is this my horse?" Jenny tugged her hat farther down on her head, then pulled on her gloves.

Luke nodded. "Missy's pretty gentle, but she's got spirit, too. If you're as good a rider as you claim, I don't think you'll get bored." He walked to his horse, but not before he saw sparks ignite in her eyes. When he reached his gelding, he checked the cinch again, and glanced up to find Jenny adjusting the length of her stirrups.

He gave his daughter a boost up onto her mount, then watched Garrett climb easily onto Willie. He felt an ache throughout his body when Jenny stuck her booted foot in the stirrup and swung her slender jean-clad leg over the horse. With a tug on the reins, she maneuvered Missy once around the corral, taking the mare through her commands. Then she stopped in front of him, a big smile on her face. "I'm ready."

Luke's body tensed. Yeah, he was ready, too. More than ready.

"Okay, let's go," Garrett called. He kicked his pony's flank, leading the foursome out of the corral. Jenny followed behind Crissy, and Luke fell in last.

Their destination was a secret between father and son. Jenny was willing to go anywhere today, she thought, busy taking in all the beautiful scenery. The endless blue sky, rolling green hills, the grandeur of the Big Horn Mountains.

Luke rode up beside her. "How ya doin'?"

"Great. It's so beautiful. Is all this yours?"

"About sixty thousand acres." Luke pointed toward the mountains. "Prime ranch land that goes all the way to the foothills. There are two large creeks that run across the middle of the property and an abundance of wildlife."

"You hunt?"

Again he nodded. "Antelope, elk, deer.... In the fall, I hire out as a scout." He gave her a sideways glance. "Do you have a problem with that?"

She shook her head. "Only if you kill for the trophy."

"I don't." He shifted in the saddle. "Now, the men who hire me...that's their business. But I've been offered the carcass more than once."

"I went hunting with my brothers once." She looked at Luke as he guided his gelding beside her. There was no doubt the man was at home around horses. "I didn't like it much."

"The extra money helps to keep the ranch going during the rough times." He sighed. "And I seem to have had a lot of those lately."

"Don't you have any help?"

"I hire on a part-timer during roundup, but usually I handle things on my own."

"So Drew doesn't help at all?"

He tossed her a crooked smile and her heart leaped. "Whatever gave you the idea that he did?" he teased.

Jenny couldn't resist and she smiled, too. "Oh, just something I picked up on the last time you stopped by the courthouse." And I almost had to stop a fight, she added silently. "Why can't you two get along?"

Luke sobered and shifted in the saddle. "Drew wasn't raised on the ranch. He was only nine when our mother died. Because he was so young, Dad sent him into town to live with our aunt and uncle. I was older, so I stayed. While

Drew was living a pampered life in town, I was out here working the Double R.

"We may be brothers, but we are entirely different. So different that he wants nothing to do with the ranch outside of selling the land. I never will, and Drew knows it. Now he's going after the mineral rights so he can bring in a company to drill." Luke pulled off his hat and wiped his forehead with his sleeve. "I'll never agree to that, no matter how many lawyers he gets." There was no mistaking the anger in his tone.

"Maybe if the two of you could sit down and discuss this..."

Luke glared at her. "We have. Drew wants to sell—I don't."

So both Reillys were stubborn, Jenny thought. "Maybe if you—"

"Maybe we better not talk about this anymore," he interrupted.

Jenny hesitated only a second, then nodded. Luke was right. She was nosing into something that wasn't her business.

All at once, Garrett was beside her. "Jenny. I'll race you to those trees."

"Sure. I'll even give you a head start." Jenny pulled her hat down on her head.

Garrett took off on Willie and Jenny waited until he had a pretty good lead. That's when Luke said, "Don't make it so easy for him." Suddenly, he reached across and smacked her mare on the rump.

Jenny was caught off guard as her horse took off, but with her years of riding, she quickly got the rhythm of the mare and went after Garrett. She glanced over her shoulder and discovered Luke close on her heels.

So he wanted to race, too.

Jenny forgot about Garrett and Willie as she lowered her head to whisper encouragement to her mare, hoping to spur the animal on. Missy liked to run and was doing a good job, but Luke was gaining. Fast. Suddenly, he was next to her. He tossed her a wink and kicked his horse's sides and the animal raced ahead.

Luke won, but not by much. They slowed their horses, then finally stopped by a large stream. He climbed down and came over to Jenny. She was surprised when he helped her off Missy. Right into his arms.

"You're a damn good rider," he admitted. Their bodies brushed as he slowly lowered her to the ground and a wonderful tingle rushed through her body.

"I . . . ah, I had to be to keep up with my brothers."

His coffee eyes flickered with interest. "I bet you did a good job."

"I tried hard enough."

"Don't like to lose, huh?"

The sound of the kids coming drew them apart. "Boy, Jenny, that was neat," Garrett said excitedly as he climbed off Willie. "You almost beat Dad. Nobody beats him. Huh, Dad?"

"Not recently," Luke answered as he helped Crissy off Calico.

"When are we going to eat lunch?" Crissy asked. "I'm hungry."

"Pretty soon, honey." Luke tugged playfully at his daughter's hat, then gathered the horses' reins and walked the animals to the creek for a drink. Mounting the horses again, they crossed at a shallow spot and went another quarter mile before ending up at a grassy cove shaded by a large grove of trees.

"Oh, my. This looks like paradise." Jenny sighed.

"It's called Lost Pony Cove," Luke said.

"That's what the Indians named it," Garrett explained. "The Indians used to try and capture wild ponies by running them in here." The boy pointed behind him. "They thought they'd have them trapped. But the ponies would escape through a secret passage way back in the hills. Isn't that true, Dad?"

"Pretty close, son." Luke untied the rolled blanket and saddlebag from his daughter's horse. He walked to a big tree and spread it out on the ground.

"I wrote about Lost Pony Cove for school," Crissy offered.

"Must be great being around all this history," Jenny said.

"Great for school projects," Luke said as he invited her to sit on the blanket. He opened the saddlebag and glanced inside. "Now, we have peanut butter and jelly, or ham and cheese sandwiches. We also have chips and apples and bananas." He smiled and Jenny's breath caught. "And for dessert, Crissy made chocolate brownies."

"I helped, too," Garrett said enthusiastically.

"Well, those are all my favorites," Jenny admitted. "Especially chocolate brownies."

Luke sat back and watched as his son took the spot next to Jenny. It didn't surprise him. Garrett hadn't talked about much else since the woman had come to Last Hope. His gaze roamed over the beautiful brunette with the bedroom eyes who had managed to keep his mind pretty occupied the past few weeks, as well.

"I made the peanut butter ones," Garrett said.

Jenny looked perplexed for a second. "Well, then, I'll eat one of your sandwiches and Crissy's brownies." She raised her gaze to meet his and smiled innocently. "What do you want, Luke?"

He bit back a groan. Did she have any idea what she was doing to him? "I'll have a ham and cheese." He reached inside the saddlebag and pulled out canned sodas for everyone.

The meal was filled with excited chatter from Garrett. Crissy was quiet, but Jenny managed to get her to talk a bit. Luke lay down on the blanket and pulled his hat over his face, relaxing in the warm sun.

Jenny stared at the man lying on the blanket, sound asleep. It had been over an hour since Luke dozed off. She and the kids had gone on a hike, but she wouldn't let them wander too far since she didn't know the area. Now, both Crissy and Garrett were playing at the edge of the stream, with strict orders not to go in the water.

It was past four o'clock and they needed to head back to the ranch. She hated to wake Luke. She tried taking his hat off his face, but he just rolled over on his side and murmured something incoherent. Jenny sighed in frustration, but soon found herself eagerly studying his long lean body, from his narrow hips, over his flat stomach, all the way to his wide shoulders. There was dark stubble just starting to appear on his stubborn chin. He had well-shaped eyebrows and long to-die-for black lashes. Then Luke's mouth drew her attention, remembering the touch of his lips had been a delicious sensation.

The kids' voices broke into Jenny's thoughts. *Pull yourself together girl, you're getting carried away about a man who usually doesn't want to give you the time of day.*

Jenny drew another breath and released it slowly. Well, staring at the man wasn't going to wake him up. She placed her hand on Luke's arm. "Luke, wake up. It's getting late."

It took a second or two for Luke to get his bearings. He blinked and the first thing to come into focus was Jenny's face. He raised onto his elbow, and she smiled. "Did you have a nice nap?"

"Yeah, it was great." He rubbed his hand over his face. "I'm sorry, I didn't mean to leave you with the kids."

"It's okay. I enjoyed myself. We went for a short hike and now they're looking for arrowheads along the bank. I just thought maybe we should be heading back to the ranch."

He sat up and draped his arm over his raised knee. "Sure," he said with a lot more enthusiasm than he felt. Jeez . . . he must have slept like the dead. "Give me a minute." He glanced up and realized how close she was, and his heart raced.

"Take your time. I just didn't know how long it would take to get back." She started to get up, but he reached for her, finding he wanted her to stay right where she was.

"We have plenty of daylight. The ride back will only take about fifteen minutes. We took the scenic route out here."

Her eyes glowed. "Thanks for a wonderful day."

"It wasn't a big deal." He shrugged. But it was turning into one, he thought. He hadn't been able to stop the ache in his gut since she'd walked into the barn earlier, or control the way his body responded to her just being near.

"Dad! Dad! Look what I found," Garrett yelled as he came running toward them. The boy dived onto the blanket and nearly fell over Jenny. "I think it's a arrowhead."

Welcoming his son's interruption, he took the flat object from Garrett. "Let me see." Luke caught a whiff of Jenny's perfume when she leaned closer to look, too. He couldn't handle it. He climbed to his feet and walked out into the sunlight.

Garrett followed. "Is it, Dad?"

"Not sure, son. Maybe we better take it home so we can examine it closer. Let's get packed up—" He stopped, seeing that everything except for the blanket, had been put away in the saddlebags.

He shot a surprised glance at Jenny. "Looks like you've been busy."

She shrugged. "The kids helped. I promised them another game of Monopoly tonight, but...if you're busy or something, we can make it another time."

He shook his head. "I just figured you'd had your fill of us for one day."

She tilted her head slightly. "Oh, no. I've been having a great time. I like having kids around."

"Stay for supper, then. Crissy and Garrett can play a short game before bedtime."

"Yeah, Jenny," Garrett cheered. "Stay for supper."

Jenny seemed bewildered. "You want me to?"

More than he should, Luke thought. "Yeah, I do."

He grabbed the blanket and rolled it up, then tied it to his horse. He got the kids mounted and they all started back.

In twenty minutes, they made it to the ranch. Luke led the horses into the barn while Jenny took the children into the house.

Once inside the kitchen, Garrett charged off to get the board game. Jenny set it aside and talked the two into helping put together dinner. She had Garrett set the table and Crissy chop the lettuce and tomatoes. By the time Luke walked in the door, everything was ready.

"I didn't mean for you to cook the meal."

Jenny couldn't tell if he was angry. "It wasn't that hard. Besides, it's only tacos." She shrugged. In fact, she'd enjoyed it, since she hadn't cooked much lately. "And Crissy and Garrett helped me." She took a pot holder, opened the oven and pulled out the foil-wrapped tortillas. Setting them on the table, she announced, "Supper."

The children quickly took their seats, and Jenny pulled out the chair next to Garrett. She watched as Luke sat at the head of the table. They bowed their heads and said a blessing, then she picked up the tortillas, took one and passed the plate to Garrett.

"Wasn't today neat, Dad?" Garrett handed his dad the plate. "It was like a real family."

"But I don't want to go to sleep. I'm not tired," Garrett said, yawning.

"Well, I am," Jenny said. "So roll over, and I'll rub your back. That'll help."

"I don't want to 'cause you'll go home."

Jenny felt her throat tighten. "Honey, I have to go back to my apartment in town. I have to go to work in the morning."

"But can't you work here? Then you can be here all the time."

"Oh, that would be fun, honey, but I already have a job."
And I doubt that your dad would like me as the house-
keeper, she thought.

"Garrett." Luke's stern voice filled the bedroom. "It's
well past your bedtime. So say good-night to Jenny."

"Okay." The boy threw his arms around her and kissed
her cheek. " 'Night, Jenny. Thanks for coming today." His
arms tightened around her neck. "Will you come back?"

"Sure, and maybe you can come into town and see me."

The boy nodded, then rolled to his side. Jenny pulled the
blankets up, placed another kiss on his cheek and left the
room. She went down the hall and said good-night to Crissy
who was reading in bed. Luke, too, kissed his daughter and
made her promise to turn out the light in thirty minutes.

After checking on Garrett once more, Jenny went downstairs where she found Luke in front of the hearth, stoking
the fire.

"It's cooled down outside. Could you stay a while?" he
asked as he stood and came across the room.

Jenny's heart was racing as he reached for her hand. She
shouldn't, but she wasn't listening to her common sense
right now. "Maybe for a little while. I have a long drive to
town."

"A long ... cold drive." He led her to the sofa and they
both sat down.

"Then maybe I better get started," she argued weakly,
knowing she really didn't want to go ... yet.

"How 'bout I warm you up a little before you go out in
the cold?"

Luke seemed to know exactly what he wanted when he
pulled her into his arms and lowered his mouth to hers. He
kissed her softly at first, as if testing, then with a murmur
of satisfaction, deeper, so that her lips parted to receive him.
Jenny's calm was quickly shattered by the raw hunger of his
kiss. She was shocked at her own eager response to the man.

He drew back slightly, then taking teasing little nibbles
from her mouth, he shifted her onto his lap. Jenny slid her

arms around his neck and combed her fingers through his hair. Her open mouth slanted over his, wanting more. She got her wish, hearing a deep throaty sound from Luke as he pushed her down on the sofa.

Finally, he broke off the kiss and his dark gaze raked over her face. "Damn! You're beautiful." His shaky hand traced her jaw, then he took her mouth in another devouring kiss.

The woman in Luke's arms had him hot and ready. Her soft pliant body under his nearly made him crazy. He wasn't thinking about anything but how much he wanted her. His hands shifted to her breasts, filling them with their softness.

Jenny broke off the kiss. "Oh, Luke," she said with a hoarse sound that almost sent him over the edge.

"That's it, baby," he encouraged. "Make those sexy purrs for me." He started tugging her blouse from her jeans, then the phone rang.

With a string of curses, Luke climbed off the sofa and hurried to the desk. "Double R," he grumbled into the receiver.

"Luke, it's Drew. I'm looking for Jenny. Is she there?"

Luke closed his eyes and rubbed his hand over his face. Damn his brother. "Yeah." He held out the phone to Jenny. "For you. It's Drew."

Embarrassed about what had nearly happened, Jenny stood and took the receiver from Luke. She brushed her hair from her face. "Hello, Drew. What's wrong?"

"I've been looking for you all day."

She glanced at Luke, seeing him pace across the room. "What's so important you needed to get hold of me on Sunday?"

"I wanted to remind you we have a city council meeting in the morning," Drew said. "Eight o'clock sharp."

Jenny knew about the meeting; Ruth had told her on Friday. "I'll be there, Drew."

"Are you all right, Jenny? You sound strange. You want me to drive out and get you?"

She sighed in frustration. Did she look helpless? she wondered. "No, Drew, I'm fine. See you tomorrow." She hung up before he could say anything more. She looked at Luke. "Drew wanted to remind me about tomorrow's meeting."

"I didn't know your job required you to give your whereabouts twenty-four hours a day."

"It doesn't. He was just concerned—"

"The hell he was. The man was checking up on you."

She crossed her arms defensively. This sounded like the conversation she'd had with her brother Tyler earlier today. "What if he was?"

"It just seems to me that you have a pretty close relationship with your boss."

"I do not," she denied.

"Then why was he calling here to find you? He could have left a message on your answering machine," he said, raising an eyebrow. "Or maybe you two have more going on than business."

Jenny marched to the closet and pulled out her jacket. She wasn't going to hang around to hear any more. To think she was starting to care for this man. She blinked back tears as she jammed her arms into her coat.

"Where are you going?"

"Somewhere I don't have to listen to your insults."

He grabbed her by the arm. "Just tell me one thing, Jenny. What's going on between you and Drew?"

The hurt she felt was like a gash through her heart as her gaze drifted to the sofa. How could he think that, after...?

She raised her chin to meet his accusing gaze. "You tell me, Luke. You seem to have all the answers." She jerked from his hold and walked out the door.

Chapter Seven

Luke was angry, more with himself than anybody else. He'd broken a promise. He'd let a woman get under his skin.

He released a long sigh as he drove his blue Bronco toward the ranch. It was after six and he was tired and hungry. He'd spent the last three days sitting in a saddle, rounding up cattle for the spring branding. He'd barely managed four hours of sleep a night. His back hurt from tangling with too many ornery calves, and he'd even gotten kicked in the shins, which had left a big bruise and a helluva sore leg.

Taking care of the kids and running the Double R should be enough distraction to keep him from thinking of one petite brunette, whose beautiful brown eyes had been haunting him night after night. But all the physical activity in the world hadn't gotten Jenny Murdock out of his head.

The past week he'd laid awake, thinking about the kisses they'd shared in front of the fire. Her sweet mouth...her sweet body. His pulse began to race and he nearly missed the turnoff to the ranch.

"Damn!" he cursed, and jerked the wheel sharply. "I don't need this." He parked the car and ran his hand through his hair. There was no denying it. There was definitely an attraction between them, purely physical, of course. Hell, why not? He was only thirty-three, and he had needs. Needs he thought had died after Cindy left him. He was wrong. Jenny made him realize that he was very much a man. And he'd come to the stark realization that he wanted to spend time with her.

A broad grin crossed his face. Maybe a little socializing wouldn't be such a bad idea. It didn't have to lead anywhere if he didn't want it to. He got out of the truck and started toward the house, a bit more spring to his step.

Jenny tucked the phone against her ear and sifted through the pile of papers on her desk. "Yes, Pastor Wilson. I'm glad we were able to agree on a date. I can't tell you how much I'm looking forward to working with Mrs. Wilson on this social." She nodded. "Sure ... ah, Tuesday afternoon will be fine. Thanks again. Goodbye." She hung up the phone and quickly circled the date on her calendar.

A big grin appeared as she jumped up from her desk. "I did it!" She began dancing around her small office. "I did it," she cheered again. The door opened and Ruth walked in.

"Don't look now, Jenny, but I think your job is getting to you."

"And I love it," Jenny agreed. "The first social is scheduled for June fourth."

"That's great. So you finally talked old Pastor Wilson into letting you use the church hall?"

"Yes, the church guild is in charge of the food and drinks—that means no alcohol whatsoever."

"Probably just as well, there'll be less trouble if the men aren't drinking. Though I never minded men fighting over me. I suspect you don't, either." Ruth slowly shook her head. "Huh, only in town a month and already got two men's attention."

"What are you talking about?"

"The Reilly brothers, of course."

"What!" Jenny stared at the woman in disbelief. "Are you crazy? I can't... believe that you would say that. Does everyone think there's something going on?"

"People are a little curious, it's only natural. Jenny, you're a pretty woman. You're bound to have a few men sniffing around you. You're just lucky enough to have two handsome brothers fighting for your attention."

"Drew and I work together, I'm his assistant. How else am I supposed to do my job?"

Ruth quickly raised her hand. "I know you two aren't dating, or anything. I'm saying that I think Drew would be happy with more."

Jenny shook her head. "There isn't going to be more. He's just a good friend."

Ruth arched an eyebrow. "How about Luke?"

Jenny's stomach knotted, recalling the scene at the ranch. "Definitely not," she said adamantly. Her anger had faded over the past five days, but not the hurt. To her dismay, the fact that she couldn't seem to get the man out of her mind made her realize that she cared.

"Too bad, you'd be good for Luke. That is, if he let you get close enough."

Jenny swung around. "I already told you, Ruth. There is no Luke and I."

"My, methinks thou doth protest too much," Ruth teased, but quickly grew serious. "Just understand, Luke's wife hurt him bad. It's been a few years, but she left some pretty deep scars."

Jenny stared at her friend, wanting to hear more, but the phone rang. She picked it up.

"Mayor Reilly's office. Jenny Murdock speaking."

"Hi, honey."

"Mom. Is everything okay?" Jenny sat on the edge of her desk and looked up to see Ruth give a silent wave and leave.

"Everything's fine. Can't a mother call her only daughter if she feels like it?"

"As long as there isn't something you're not telling me." It had been nearly two years since her father's death, and Jenny knew how devastating losing J.T. had been for her mother, for the entire family. Her parents had had a wonderful relationship. After twenty-nine years of marriage, they'd still acted like newlyweds. Someday, Jenny hoped to have the same kind of marriage.

"Well, there is, in a way," Caroline said. "Brett might be up your way in the next few weeks. He's going to be looking over some land for testing."

"Really? Is Jessie coming, too?"

"No, it's a quick trip. I just didn't want you to feel that we were sending him there to check up on you."

"Mother, are you trying to ease your conscience?"

"Believe me, Jen, if I were checking up on you, I'd send Tyler. But I'm keeping my promise to leave you alone for six months."

Jenny laughed. "Thanks for that."

"Just take care, honey. Remember, I love you. Here's Ty."

"Love you, too. Bye, Mom."

"Just because I'm not coming with Brett doesn't mean I'm resigned to your living there." Her brother's booming voice rang loud and clear.

"Hello to you, too, Ty. And, yes, I'm fine. How's the family?"

"We'd be better if you'd come home and forget this foolishness."

"It's not foolish. I have a great job and I'm living my life. C'mon, Ty, it's time I stopped leaning on you. You have to let me go, too. You have Maggie and the kids."

Luke hadn't planned on eavesdropping. But Jenny's door was open, and he couldn't help overhearing the phone conversation.

"I love you, too," she said in a velvety voice that had Luke gripping the doorknob like a vise. Murderous thoughts raced through his head.

Then, as if Jenny sensed his presence, she looked up. She continued to carry on the conversation, but her mesmerizing gaze was on him. Days of not seeing her made him hungry for the sight of her as his eyes traveled up her shapely legs that were draped over the edge of the desk, then to the navy skirt hugging the sweet curves of her hips. A prim cream-colored blouse was buttoned to the neck, where she was wearing an oval pin at the collar. Her hair was clipped back, lying against her shoulders in curls, soft touchable curls.

"Look," she said into the receiver, "someone just came in. I'll have to go. Bye."

Jenny replaced the receiver and stood up from the desk, but her suddenly weak legs refused to move. All she managed to do was stare at the way Luke's white shirt fit across his broad shoulders, and register the fact that his jeans should be labeled indecent, the way they fit his narrow hips and long muscular legs. Suddenly, she was having trouble breathing.

"Luke," she said finally, "if you're here to see Drew, he's out for most of the day."

"I know," he said and walked into her office. "I came to see you."

"Me? Why?"

"That all depends." He nodded toward the phone. "How important is that man to you?"

Jenny frowned. What was he talking about? "You mean—"

"Hell, I don't care what his name is," Luke swiftly interrupted. "Are you involved with him?"

All at once, it dawned on Jenny what he was thinking. She wanted to smile and she did. "Yes, I'm involved. And yes, he's very important to me, has been for a long time."

Luke's deep-set eyes flashed with anger. "Hell, Jenny, doesn't it even matter that the man is married?"

She sat back down on the desk to enjoy this. "But I knew him before he was married."

Luke let go with some colorful expletives. "Is he the reason you left Texas?"

"He's one of them."

"Dammit, Jenny. Forget him." Luke started pacing in front of her. "It's not going to lead anywhere."

"I can't forget him, Luke, believe me, I've tried."

He looked defeated as he walked to the door. "Well, then, I guess there's nothing left to say."

Jenny knew she should let him go, let him think the worst and maybe the man would leave her alone. But, in her heart, she knew she didn't want him to.

"Tyler Murdock may be bullheaded, stubborn and he sticks his nose into my life more than I like, but I love him for caring," she called through the door.

Luke peered back into the room. He looked embarrassed. "The man on the phone was your brother?"

She nodded and her smile brightened.

"You enjoyed letting me make a fool of myself."

Jenny sobered. "You're the one who's always jumping to conclusions about me."

Luke watched the hurt play across her face. He felt like a heel knowing he'd been the cause. "Jenny..." He started toward her, then stopped. He needed to keep his distance. "About the other night... I know I said some lousy things to you. I'm... sorry." His eyes met hers, hoping to find warmth and understanding, and maybe a touch of desire.

"I guess it's understandable to be jealous of your brother."

"I am not jealous of Drew," he insisted. "Unless you choose him over me." This time, he took that step and reached out to touch her cheek. "Then I would have to convince you to change your mind." His voice was husky as he started to lower his head.

Jenny stopped him. "Maybe this isn't such a good idea, Luke."

He tilted her chin upward and caught the heavenly fragrance of her perfume. "You're probably right. But there's something between us, Jenny. You know it and I know it. I'm not sure where it's going to lead, but I do know I want to spend time with you."

This was a big mistake, Jenny decided as she and Luke walked into Molly's fifteen minutes later. Everyone in the place turned and eyed them closely when Luke placed his hand on her back and guided her to a booth by the window.

"Sorry, I guess I should have chosen another place. But I have to pick up Garrett at his friend's in an hour."

"I wondered where he was."

"Did you think I left him at the ranch?"

"No, I didn't. You're too good a father to leave your children, even for a short time."

"Believe me, there are times when I'd like to."

"Isn't there someone who can help you? Any day-care centers?"

He shook his head. "A few of the churches run child-care facilities, but it's mostly mothers taking turns watching the kids. Molly and Tom have taken Crissy and Garrett on occasion, but I really hate to ask unless it's an emergency."

"Well, if you want, I'd love to spend time with Crissy and Garrett. Of course, it would have to be on a weekend."

He tossed her a sexy grin and her heart turned over in response. "You'd do that?"

"Sure. I used to take care of my niece, Becky. Ty was a single parent for a while, so I know it's hard to get anything done with a five-year-old tagging along."

"There's no doubt that Garrett is a handful. I've been wanting to get the work started on the new barn."

"What's wrong with the one you have now?"

"Nothing. I'm planning on expanding my horse-boarding business. Later on, maybe starting a riding stable."

She folded her hands on the table. "Oh, how exciting."

"Not unless I get a second barn. Since I have two mares ready to foal, I've got to get something together before winter." He cocked an eyebrow. "You any good at barn raisings?"

"Sure. They're a lot of fun. I went to one in Oklahoma for my brother Brett and his wife, Jessie."

He leaned back in the booth, and a mischievous glint appeared in his eye. "You're a confusing woman, Jenny Murdock."

"How's that?" she asked.

"You seem so close to your family. I can't figure out why you decided to come all the way to Wyoming."

To be me, she wanted to shout. Not just Jennifer Murdock, daughter of Texas oil tycoon, J.T. Murdock. "I'll have to introduce you to my brothers to make you understand. They've been trying to run my life for the past twenty-six years."

Luke smiled, knowing she probably didn't make it easy for them, either. "I bet they've had their hands full, too."

"They only got what they deserved." Her mouth lifted at the corners, and he felt the urge to kiss her. "But I managed to get even."

"I bet you did." It was easy to talk with her. "How do they feel about your going off and looking for a husband?" he teased, and watched her eyes flash.

"I told you, I never said I was looking for a husband."

"Well, sweetheart, nearly everyone in town is looking at you. There wasn't a man at the counter who didn't turn around when you walked in." Luke knew it was only a matter of time before someone snatched her up. What bothered him the most was the idea that it would more than likely be Drew.

Five days later, Jenny hung the last of the colorful paper decorations in Shelly's sixth-grade classroom. In less than twenty minutes, there would be thirty-five students and their parents invading the small room for the-end-of-the-school-year program. Jenny had graciously offered to help her new friend with the project. In turn, Shelly had promised to come to each one of Jenny's social events.

"You think we have enough food?" Shelly asked.

Jenny eyed the long table overflowing with several different kinds of cookies, fudge and brownies. "More than enough."

Shelly frowned. "Remember, my students' families are coming, too. Younger brothers and sisters can clear off a table in the blink of an eye."

"I could stand guard and smack their fingers with a ruler if they take too many," Jenny teased.

Shelly stiffened. "I don't have a classroom filled with angels, but I haven't lost my temper enough to strike a child. I never will."

Jenny caught a strange sadness in her friend's eyes before she walked back to her desk.

"I'm sorry, Shelly, I was only teasing. I've never struck a child in my life, except for Billy Howe in third grade. I love kids."

Shelly turned around. "I know, Jenny. I'm sorry. Sometimes I get on my soapbox before I realize what I'm doing. It's just that I've seen so many children that were..." She drew a long breath. "In Kansas City, I taught in a rough section of town. There were drug dealers on nearly every corner and so much violence. And the kids are the ones who get caught in the crossfire." More pain appeared on Shelly's face. "I couldn't take it anymore. That's the main reason I applied for a job here."

Jenny crossed the room to comfort her. "I'm glad you did. The kids in Last Hope need you."

A sudden noisy commotion drew them to their stations as the students filed into the room. Jenny took her place by the refreshments and searched the crowd for Crissy, but mostly she was looking for Luke.

Jenny had had a busy week, but she'd expected to at least hear from him. But not even a phone call since he had taken her to lunch. What had she done wrong? He was the one who'd said he wanted to spend time with her.

She glanced at the doorway and got her wish. His hair was still damp and combed off his forehead. He was holding his hat in one hand and his daughter's in the other. Behind him, Garrett came into the room and made a dash for the refreshment table.

"Jenny!" He looked shocked to see her. "Are you a teacher now?"

Jenny giggled as she hugged the small boy. "No, silly. I'm just helping Ms. Hart."

"Crissy says she the best teacher in the whole school. I hope I get her when I go next year."

"Well, you'll have to start with Mrs. Earl in kindergarten. I hear she's pretty good, too."

The boy looked sad. "Jenny, why haven't you come to the ranch again?"

"You know I've been working for your uncle Drew. Sometimes my job takes a lot of time."

"But can't you come on Sunday again?" Garrett pleaded. "You don't work that day."

No, she didn't. But did Luke want her around? "I'm not sure, Garrett." She wasn't about to force herself on the man and his family. "Maybe you can come into town and spend the day with me."

"You don't like going riding at the ranch?"

Luke's voice brought her eyes up to meet his. She drew a long breath to calm her racing heart. "I love to ride." Her voice softened. "I guess I was just waiting for an invitation."

"I thought my son just asked you."

Jenny's eyes darted back to Garrett's expectant look. "Honey, would you watch the table for a minute? I need to talk to your father."

"Sure." The boy's eyes lit up as he hurried behind the table.

Jenny went out into the hall followed by Luke. In the midst of the confusion of students and their parents, she managed to find a quiet corner. When she raised her eyes to meet Luke's gaze, she nearly lost her nerve. "There's no need for you to feel that you have to have me out to the ranch. Just because Garrett wants—"

"Jenny," he cut her off. "I told you before, you can ride anytime you want."

The same way you said you wanted to spend time with me, she thought. "Thanks, but maybe it's not such a good idea." She started to walk back and he grabbed her by the arm.

"What's that supposed to mean?"

His dark eyes bore into hers, making her more nervous than she wanted to admit. "I didn't want you to feel obligated just because you took me to lunch. And since you didn't call..."

He released her. "Look, I can't just drop everything. I have a ranch to run and kids to raise...." He raked his hand through his hair in frustration as he glanced around. "Hell, this is crazy. I've got to go." He took off, leaving her standing there gaping.

"Then just go, Luke Reilly," Jenny murmured, watching as he went back into the classroom. "See if I care," she said, feeling the slow ache grip her heart. But it was too late. She already did care.

* * *

The following week was a busy one. But finally, when things had calmed down, Jenny had been taking advantage of the peace. She'd caught up on her correspondence, and had gone over the last-minute preparations for the mixer on Friday.

Now she was working on a new project she wanted to present to Drew, but decided it might be best if she waited to see how successful the dance turned out. The young mayor had been good about letting her have a free hand in organizing all social events in Last Hope.

Shelly had helped, too. They'd both attended services at the small Calvary Church on Sunday and Pastor Wilson had introduced her to some of the parishioners who would be helping her. Jenny also met several unattached men who were eager to attend Friday night's event. More and more, she was finding the small community of Last Hope a friendly place. Of course, a few were leery of her motives.

Luke came to mind. Darn! Why couldn't she get the man out of her head? She hadn't seen him in over a week, but every time she turned around, he'd intruded into her thoughts. Maybe at the social, she might find someone...

Suddenly, she heard voices, loud voices, reverberating from the empty corridor outside her office. If she could hear it, so could everyone else. Jenny walked into the hall, where she found Luke and Drew arguing, neither seeming to care who heard them.

Jenny did. She hurried to them, stepping between the angry brothers. "Why don't you two go inside and discuss this, so the whole town doesn't know your private business?" She pointed to the mayor's office and waited.

The brothers continued to glare at each other, then Drew turned and walked inside. Luke hesitated, then slowly followed. Jenny boldly went in, too, and closed the door.

"Okay, what got you two so fired up?"

Luke darted her a fierce look, but she ignored it.

"You can't go around yelling at each other all the time," she began. "It's childish, for one thing." She flashed a knowing look between the brothers, but they refused to meet her gaze. "Whatever this problem is, it's time you two try to work it out."

"How can I?" Drew began. "Luke won't even listen to what I have to say. He thinks the ranch is his. Well, I've got news for you, bro, I own half."

"You never cared at all until someone approached you about the mineral rights," Luke challenged, then glanced at Jenny. "I don't want to discuss this now. But one last thing..." Luke waved a piece of paper in his brother's face. "If you think this is going to scare me into having the testing done, you're crazy."

"It's half mine. At least I should have a say about having a geological survey done."

Luke's expression grew fierce. "Over my dead body."

"That can be arranged." Drew jolted back.

"Stop it." Jenny shouted. "This isn't getting you anywhere. There's got to be a way both of you can have what you want."

"There is," Drew said. "We're going to court."

"No court is going to tell me what to do with my land."

Jenny put her hands up again. She saw the pain in Luke's face. But she knew that the courts could take it out of their hands. He might lose everything.

"Luke, Drew's right. You two have to come to an understanding." She took a calming breath. "Can't you do both? Let a survey crew come out and at least see if there are any mineral deposits on the property. Maybe you can come to terms on something."

Luke flashed her a look of disdain. "You had me fooled, Jenny Murdock. I thought maybe you were different. But money is the key factor here, isn't it? Everybody is always looking for the almighty buck." He nodded at his brother. "Well, maybe you two deserve each other." He opened the door and stalked out.

"Wait, Luke." Jenny started after him, but Drew grabbed her arm.

"Let him go. He's always been hotheaded about the ranch, but he's not getting away with it anymore. That's what we're going to court over."

"But, Drew, you can't take Luke to court, He's your brother."

"What else is there? He won't listen. I've tried, but he looks at everything as if a it's a competition between us. And since you came to work for me, he's even more jealous."

"Why?"

"C'mon, Jenny. Luke hates the fact that I'm with you all day."

He stepped closer, and Jenny tensed, knowing he wanted to kiss her.

"Drew, this isn't a good idea," she hedged.

"But, why can't we, Jenny? Why can't we have more—"

Jenny raised her hand to stop his words. "Because, Drew. We can't."

Looking defeated, he dropped his hand to his side. "Jenny, you haven't even given it a chance."

"Over the past couple of months, I've loved working for you and have treasured the time we've spent together, becoming *friends*." She waited to see his reaction, wondering why she couldn't feel more for the man. "Believe me, Drew, I don't want to lose that."

"I guess I don't, either," he agreed. Then he asked, "Is it because of Luke?"

Jenny couldn't deny it anymore. "Yes, I have feelings for your brother. And I'm going out to the ranch to see if I can talk some sense into him." She started for the door.

"It's a lost cause," Drew called after her.

Jenny didn't think so. She might be able to reason with him. But breaking down the wall around Luke's heart might take a lot more work.

Chapter Eight

Jenny slammed her car door and marched toward the ranch house, determined not to let Luke walk away from her. This time, he was going to listen to what she had to say, even if she had to tie him down, she swore to herself as she climbed the porch steps. But before she had a chance to knock on the door, she heard her name called.

She swung around and saw Crissy and Garrett running from the barn.

"Daddy needs help," Garrett yelled.

Jenny's heart began to race. "Is he hurt?"

"No." Crissy shook her head as she tried to catch her breath. "It's Sassy. She's having trouble with her foal. Dad told me to call Doc Peters."

"Do as he says, Crissy." Jenny hugged both children. "Then stay in the house so you won't be in the way."

"Will you stay with us?" Garrett asked.

"No, I've got to help your dad. Now, go on inside." She nudged them toward the house. "We'll let you know when the new colt is here." Praying that was true, she raced to the barn.

As she approached the back stall, she heard the neighing sound of the roan mare. The animal was already down and obviously in labor. Jenny quickly knelt next to Sassy's head and rubbed the horse's sweat-covered neck in hopes of calming her.

"It's okay, girl. We're gonna help you."

Luke glanced at her. If he was surprised to see her, he didn't show it. He rolled up his shirtsleeves, then rinsed his hand in a tub of disinfectant solution.

"How long has she been in labor?" Jenny asked.

"Not sure. I checked her around five this morning. She seemed fine. I was so angry when I took off for town..." He let the words trail off as he knelt beside the horse's rump and positioned himself to examine her. "When I got home a while ago, I found her already down. Try and keep her still."

Sassy raised her head and Jenny tightened her hold.

Luke reached inside the large animal and examined her. "Damn! I think it's turned. I can't find the legs." He grimaced and beads of sweat popped out on his forehead.

Jenny wanted to help, but she knew that until he positioned the colt she couldn't do much. Besides, she was using all her strength to soothe the laboring mother.

"C'mon, hang in there, Sassy. It'll be worth it when you see your baby," Jenny said.

Luke listened to Jenny's soft voice and found himself believing her, too. In reality, he knew if he didn't get the foal out, he could lose both animals. He looked at the woman dressed in the business suit, kneeling on the straw-covered floor, cradling the frightened mare. She gave him an encouraging smile that seemed to spur him on.

"C'mon, Luke, you can do it."

It seemed like a miracle when his hand came in contact with the long bony legs. "Got 'em." He grimaced once again, until finally he worked the legs around toward the birth canal. Removing his hand, he let nature and Sassy do the rest.

Slowly, a pair of long, mucus-covered legs slid out first, then with another contraction, the mare finished the delivery. Luke stood back and watched as the rusty-colored foal dropped at his feet. No matter how many times he'd witnessed this, he was still amazed.

"Oh, he's beautiful," Jenny said.

Luke could hear the emotion in her voice, and he looked up to find tears in her eyes. Big brown eyes brimming with tenderness and...passion. He couldn't stop the strange sensations racing through him. Something more intimate had happened between them than the birthing of a foal.

Sassy got to her feet, and like a pro she tended to her chore of cleaning her colt. Luke knew he wasn't needed any longer, and after wiping his hands on a towel, he went to Jenny. He reached out and helped her up, then drew her close.

"I'm sure glad you showed up," he breathed, then his head lowered to hers. It would take a natural disaster to keep him from kissing her now.

Jenny was unable to answer when his mouth covered hers and he pulled her tight against him. She moaned as he parted her lips and his tongue stroked hers. Swiftly losing control, she curled her fingers through his hair, straining into the kiss, the heat of it, the promise...

"This is crazy," she whispered breathlessly, but praying it would never end.

"Crazy," he agreed, dragging his mouth from hers and raining kisses over her face.

Her knees trembled and threatened to give way when his hot breath reached her neck, sending shivers down her spine. "I didn't come out here for this, I... *Ooohhh.*" His tongue dipped into her ear, causing an uncontrollable reaction. Then he returned to her lips to continue his relentless assault.

Lord, the man knew how to kiss.

"Daddy, Dr. Peters is here."

They both jerked apart hearing Crissy coming into the barn. Jenny tried to straighten her blouse and brushed the straw from her skirt. She looked up at Luke just as the vet and the kids appeared. She got a sexy wink and his whispered promise of "Later."

After Dr. Peters announced that Sassy and her colt were fit, with no complications from the difficult birth, he promised to send Luke a bill. The kids took turns seeing the colt, which Garrett had named Ranger. Crissy had protested, but her father had overruled her and said he liked the name, too.

Luke talked Jenny into staying for supper. Teasingly, she said he just wanted someone to cook it. He only grinned, and heaven help her, she couldn't resist the man.

After cleaning up, she made a call to the office. Although Drew knew she had gone to the ranch, she felt she owed him an explanation, especially since she had ended up taking the afternoon off.

"What are you going cook?" Garrett asked as he climbed up to the table, his familiar Power Ranger figures in his hands.

"Oh, I don't know. What would you like?"

The five-year-old looked thoughtful. "Something with mashed potatoes and gravy. Dad doesn't do that very good, and Crissy cries when hers are lumpy."

Jenny poked her head in the refrigerator and pulled open the meat drawer. There was a lot of hamburger, hot dogs and one package of chicken. "How about fried chicken?"

"Yeah," he cheered.

Jenny smiled. Garrett was so easy to please. Unlike his sister. Where was Crissy, anyway? she wondered. The girl spent a lot of time in her room. "Garrett, why don't you go and find your sister? Maybe she'd like to learn how to fry chicken."

The boy climbed down from the table. "She'll probably yell at me."

"Why?"

"'Cause she's a dumb girl."

Jenny bit her lip to keep from grinning. "Well, I'm a dumb girl too."

"No you're not," he protested. "You don't yell at me or call me a baby 'cause I don't go to school." His lip quivered. "I'm not a baby."

"No, you're not." Jenny hugged him. "In three more months, you'll be in school."

That didn't seem to satisfy the boy. "But the kids will make fun of me."

"Why?"

A tear ran down one rosy cheek, then another. "'Cause I don't have a mother."

Her own tears threatened as a sudden tightness gripped her chest. "Oh, honey." She held the small child as he began to sob. "I know how you feel, Garrett. I don't have a daddy, either. And although I miss him every day, I know there is nothing I can do to bring him back, but he will always be my daddy."

He raised his head. "But I don't remember her. I have a picture of Mom, but if I don't look at it, I can't remember what she looks like." He wiped his eyes with the back of his hands. "Since you don't have anybody, do you think maybe you could marry my dad and adopt me?"

In a minute, Jenny wanted to shout. Garrett's question caught her off guard, but it took her no time to realize there was nothing she wanted as much. Not only had she fallen in love with a stubborn cowboy with a sexy grin, she also adored his children. One problem, though, the wrong person was asking her.

"Honey, if I had a little boy, I'd want him to be just like you. But your dad has to be the one who decides if he wants to get married again. Then . . . his new wife would be your stepmother."

"What if I don't like her?" he asked. "I already like you."

"And I like you, too."

Garrett started to speak and Jenny placed her finger over his mouth. "Why don't we just agree to be friends? I promise I will be there for you. You can call me whenever you need me. Okay?"

Reluctantly, the boy nodded.

"Now, go and get your sister."

Garrett took off out of the room, and Jenny could only stand there in shock. Well, at least she'd won over one of the Reilly men. But Jenny knew the cold reality. If she ever wanted a future with Luke Reilly, she was going to have to find a way to convince him to take a chance on love again.

Luke walked into the house and was greeted with the mouth-watering aroma of fried chicken. But it was the scene in the kitchen that nearly brought him to his knees.

Jenny was standing at the stove with Crissy. Together, they were deeply engrossed in stirring the gravy. Then Jenny turned her attention to Garrett at the table. He was folding paper napkins, and placing them next to every plate. She ruffled his hair and kissed him on the cheek with praise for his accomplished task. Jenny's voice was soft and loving as she spoke to the children, her hands touching and stroking the same reassurance all the while.

Luke's heart expanded in his chest, making it difficult for him to breathe. Jenny was getting close, closer than he'd allowed anyone in a long time. He should resent her interference in his business. Instead, all he wanted to do was grab hold and take what she was offering.

He walked into the kitchen. "Looks like you've been busy,"

All heads turned toward him and smiled.

"Dad? How's Ranger?" Garrett asked as he ran to him.

"He's doing just fine," Luke said, his gaze still on Jenny. She had pulled her hair back in a braid. Her face was scrubbed clean of makeup. She was so pretty. "I checked on him right before I came in." He patted his son's shoulder, then walked to the stove.

"What are you two cooking that smells so good?"

"It's fried chicken," Crissy offered. "Jenny showed me a trick to make gravy that isn't lumpy."

His recently moody daughter looked happier than she had in days. Then he noticed her hair was pulled back in a style identical to Jenny's. "Your hair is pretty, too."

Another smile from Crissy. "Jenny showed me how to french-braid. Isn't it neat?" She turned around to show it off.

Luke looked back at Jenny. "I didn't mean for you to go to so much trouble."

"Yes, you did," Jenny teased. "And don't think I don't see through you, Luke Reilly. You and your son are pretty good at turning on your smiles and expecting women to fall at your feet and cook you supper."

As if on cue, Luke smiled. "It works with Molly, doesn't it, Garrett?"

The boy nodded. "Yep, she makes peach pie 'specially for us."

"Well, I want more than a smile."

"What did you have in mind?" Luke asked.

Jenny folded her arms over her chest. "Garrett has already promised to color me a picture to hang up in my apartment."

"Yeah, Dad, I'm going to draw one of Ranger. What are you going to do for Jenny?"

"Oh, I don't know." Luke's eyes connected with Jenny's and she blushed. He couldn't help wondering if the rosy glow covered her entire body. He stepped closer. "What do you want me to do for you, Jenny Murdock?"

Jenny backed up. "Well, I'm not sure, maybe some shelves hung up in my apartment." She stopped when she made contact with the counter. "Right now, I want you all to sit down and eat supper... it's ready."

Luke tossed her a big grin, then moved to the sink and began washing his hands. "Maybe after the kids go to bed, I can help you decide on payment."

After a long game of Monopoly and three of Go Fish, the kids were finally bathed and tucked into bed. Garrett was the last to give in, but only because Jenny said she'd come back and go riding on Sunday.

Jenny returned downstairs, but Luke was nowhere to be found. Then she heard the shower running and she knew where he'd gone. This was her chance to escape. She would be wise to climb into her car and head back to town. After the kisses in the barn earlier and the heated looks Luke had sent her during supper, she knew he had ideas of continuing tonight. It wasn't that Jenny didn't want to be in his arms, have his mouth on hers.... It was just that they had a lot of unsolved matters between them.

She looked up and found Luke standing on the stairs. He was dressed in a clean shirt and jeans that fit his tall, muscular frame sinfully. Silently, he moved in a slow easy gait across the living room and pulled her into his arms. His hands slid into her hair, turning her face up to his. Jenny wanted to protest, but where Luke Reilly was concerned, she was helpless. His mouth covered hers so quickly, so possessively, that she was incapable of denying him anything.

She released a purring sound as her arms slid around his neck and she leaned into the kiss. She soon ceased thinking and simply responded.

"You taste so good," Luke said in a husky voice. "I've wanted to do that since this afternoon."

"Maybe we shouldn't," Jenny hedged. Her common sense was returning slowly.

"You don't want this?" His teeth took teasing bites from her bottom lip, causing shivers of desire to race through her.

"Yes ... No!" She pulled back. "Luke, we shouldn't. I mean, we should talk first. The main reason I drove out to the ranch in the first place was to talk to you."

"If we start talking about what I think you want to talk about, we'll start fighting." He spoke in between nibbles along her neck. "And the last thing I want to do right now is . . . fight."

Her legs nearly gave way and she gripped his arms for support. No, she had to be strong. "Luke, I know it isn't any of my business, but I'm concerned about you and Drew . . . and the ranch."

He froze and stared at her. "I told you earlier that I'd handle it."

"I know. But I'm worried that you and your brother will grow further and further apart and you'll never come to terms."

"If you want me and Drew to get closer, you're wasting your time. We've never been close, and I don't plan on playing big brother now."

"But surely there's enough family loyalty not to want to lose the ranch."

"Look, Jenny. I don't want you involved in this." He drew a long breath. "But since you are so all fired up to do it, anyway, I might as well tell you that I'm trying to abide by our father's wishes. He's the one who didn't want anyone to drill on his land. The Double R is only one of the very few ranches in these parts that hasn't sold its mineral rights."

"Does Drew know this?" she asked.

"Drew doesn't care."

"What about you? How do you feel about it?"

"I'll do whatever it takes to keep from destroying the beauty of this land." He raised his hand in warning. "And don't say they wouldn't do that, because I've seen it happen. In a year or two, I want to open a riding stable, as soon as I get enough money together and the kids are a little older." He stepped back. "But how can I advertise horseback riding across beautiful countryside if I have oil derricks sticking up everywhere?"

Since Jenny's family were in the oil business she wanted to disagree, but didn't say anything.

"You saw the beauty of Lost Pony Cove. That could be wiped out if a company goes in there. I know with strip mining they replace everything to the way it was before, but it would be years working a mine."

You can limit the drilling, Jenny wanted to cry. *And once they take down the derrick, you can camouflage the pipes.* But she knew Luke wasn't ready to listen.

"You're right," she agreed. "Maybe we better change the subject. It's time I head back to town, anyway."

Luke drew her into his arms. "It's early."

"I've been here a long time."

"Maybe I could change your mind." He dipped his head and slanted his mouth over hers, taking her to heaven with another kiss. Jenny was breathless when he released her.

"Oh, yes. That was very convincing, Mr. Reilly. But I think it's definitely safer if I start back to town."

Luke laughed. "Maybe you're right." He hugged her tight. "But I still don't want you to go. We never get any time alone."

She had to fight hard not to weaken, and slipped out of his embrace. "Come to the dance Friday."

He cocked an eyebrow. "No way."

"Can't dance, huh?" she teased.

"I dance fine. I'm just not interested in watching a parade of potential brides."

"It's not going to be like that," she argued. "It's a social. An opportunity for single men and women to meet."

Luke tossed her a knowing look. "Sure. But count me out."

"Too bad. You're going to be missing a good time." To emphasize her words, she reached up on her toes and pulled his head down to meet hers. She put everything she had into the searing kiss as she pressed her body against his. He groaned and wrapped his arms around her, following her lead. When she released him, she caught the dangerous glint in his eyes.

Time to get out of here, she thought as she grabbed her purse and headed out the door. She climbed in the car and rolled down the window, desperately needing some cool air.

When Friday night arrived, Jenny found herself busy greeting the people filing into the church hall. Lots of people, from neighboring communities and towns had attended. She had used every means, from newspapers to local radio stations, to advertise the event. And by the looks of things, her efforts had worked.

Drew stood by her side, introducing himself to the men and women coming to the first dance.

"I can't believe how many people are here," Jenny said.

He glanced around the room. "There's still more men than women."

"It's early yet. And if word gets around, more women will come next time." Nothing was going to put a damper on her joy. She glanced across the floor and saw Shelly Hart waving at her. "Maybe we should call the next social Ladies' Choice Night and all women get in free."

"Great idea," Drew agreed. "And if they bring a female friend, they get a chance for a special door prize."

Jenny smiled. She liked the idea. "Can the budget afford it?"

Drew pursed his lips, looking amazingly like Luke. "I think so."

They both watched as the large room filled up, the women on one side, men on the other. The band had finished tuning up and announced their first song, a lively two-step. As the music began, Jenny waited to see the couples pair off. But they didn't. Not a soul got out on the floor. Jenny's stomach sank. She had to do something. If no one got together, there would be no point in a next dance.

She walked around the room to the stage. When the band finished, she got the attention of the guitar player and asked

him to make an announcement. He agreed and went back
to the microphone.

"Well, ladies, it looks like the men are a little shy tonight." The young musician grinned. "And you're gonna
have to help get things started. So I want all the men to go
out on the floor for the next dance, the John Henry."

Jenny helped nudge all the males onto the floor. The
women joined hands and eagerly made a circle around the
men.

"For those of you men who have never heard of the John
Henry, just listen for the whistle and a woman will come to
you." The band leader shook his head. "It can't get any
better than that, guys. Now, everyone have a good time."

Jenny hung the whistle around her neck and waited for
the music to start, then she gave it a hearty blow. The
women did the rest and searched out a dance partner. When
the dust settled, there were a few men left over, but not for
long. Jenny grabbed one of the men, and he eagerly two-
stepped her around the room. Not forgetting her job, she
blew the whistle and the ladies scrambled for a new partner. Jenny also found herself with another partner, a burly
man in his early thirties named Hank. The glint in his eyes
told her he was seriously looking for a woman.

She blew the whistle again and quickly sneaked off the
floor and stood next to Drew.

"You're doing a great job, Jenny."

"Thanks, boss. Why aren't you out there?"

He shrugged. "I'm not looking for anyone special."

She placed the whistle between her lips and blew hard.
"Maybe you should give it a try. That someone could be out
there."

"I doubt it." He walked away.

Jenny blew the whistle one last time and watched the large
crowd exchange partners again. She smiled. It was working.

The music changed to a ballad, and this time there wasn't
any shyness as couples began pairing off. Her thoughts

turned to Luke and she wondered what he was doing tonight. Had he been thinking about her? Had the thoughts of their kisses been keeping him awake, too?

Jenny had been pleasantly surprised when she arrived home from the ranch the other night and received a call from Luke. He said he wanted to make sure that she'd made it back to town safely.

A gentle tap on her shoulder brought her back to the present. Jenny swung around to find Luke. Her heart began to race as her hungry gaze darted over the wine-colored shirt, then to the pair of snug fitting black jeans. He looked gorgeous. "Luke, what are you doing here?"

"You invited me."

"I did, but you said that you didn't want—"

"I changed my mind," he interrupted. "Would you like to dance?"

She nodded and he led her onto the floor and took her into his arms. He smiled down at her as they moved effortlessly to the music. He even led her through several intricate turns, never missing the beat. By the end of the song, she was a little breathless. Jenny doubted it had much to do with dancing. When the band played another ballad, he pulled her close, resting his chin against her head.

Luke couldn't believe he was actually here tonight. Molly had had a lot to do with his coming. She'd made his decision easier after she had called to say she and Tom wanted to take the kids overnight. When he dropped them off, Molly had talked nonstop about the dance. Before he knew what was happening, he'd gone home, cleaned up and found himself driving back to town. He hadn't been to a dance in years.

He let his eyes drift shut as he inhaled the rosy scent of Jenny's perfume and tugged her closer. She fit perfectly in his arms, her soft curves molded to his body. God, how he'd missed her the past two days. He'd wanted so badly to call her, just to hear the husky tone of her voice.

The song ended, but Luke didn't release her. She felt too good and he wanted to hold her just a little while longer.

That wasn't to happen. Drew came by and stole her away.

"C'mon, Jenny, I need you." He pulled her from Luke's arms.

"Hey," Luke protested, "what the hell do you think you're doing?"

"We're working," Drew stated. "That's what Jenny and I are doing."

Jenny put her hand on his arm. "Luke, it's all right. The town council is hosting this mixer. We have to make some announcements."

"Let the big-time mayor make them," Luke challenged.

Drew's jaw tensed, then he turned and marched off.

"Luke, I've got to go," Jenny pleaded.

"No, you don't. Drew only came over here because you were with me. He can make the damn announcements himself. Hell, since when did he ever want to share the spotlight?"

"Please, Luke. I have to go. I'll be back later."

Luke didn't like the idea that Jenny was choosing his brother over him. "Then go."

Dammit! He didn't need this. He must have been crazy for coming here, he thought as he moved through the crowd toward the nearest exit.

Up on stage, Jenny looked around for Luke, but she couldn't find him. Reluctantly, she turned her attention to Drew as he stepped to the microphone and thanked everyone for coming. He introduced Jenny and announced the date of the next dance and the group cheered. Then to her surprise, Drew escorted her to the floor and they led off the next dance.

Jenny was angry. She had to use all her self-control to keep from stomping on Drew's foot for what he was pulling. She knew that by tomorrow everyone in town would think that they were a couple. As soon as the floor filled with dancers, she was going to excuse herself and leave the good mayor stranded.

Then she saw Luke take another woman out to the floor and Jenny's heart nearly broke in two. His pretty blond partner seemed more than eager to cuddle up in his arms.

Jenny tried to leave, but Drew insisted they finish the dance, then several other men took their turn waltzing Jenny around the floor. The painful part was having to watch Luke select partner after partner. Never once did he come back to her. Well, that was just fine. She didn't need Luke Reilly, either, or his bad attitude.

Around midnight, the band was playing the last song. A tired Jenny sat at a vacant table, her shoes off. She'd already helped clean up the food table, making sure the dishes went back to their rightful owners. She'd also thanked the Calvary Church volunteers for their help organizing the event.

She slipped on her shoes as Shelly called to her.

"Oh, Jenny, the dance was wonderful," Shelly gushed. "And so many men."

Jenny was glad her friend had had a good time. "Did you meet anyone special?"

"Yes, in fact, a group of us are going out for coffee. There's an all-night diner called Charlie's out on the highway. You want to come?"

Jenny shook her head. "I think I'll just go home to bed and sleep until Monday morning."

Shelly glanced around the nearly deserted room. "What about Luke?"

Jenny shrugged. "He probably went home." But whose home? she wondered. "And that's where I'm headed."

Shelly seemed to accept her answer and told Jenny she'd talk to her later. She and her friends went out the door.

Jenny walked to her car, hearing the laughter of couples lingering in the parking lot. Suddenly, tears formed in her eyes. Why was it so hard for her to find someone? she wondered. Was it too much to ask for a little love in her life?

She got into her car and drove the two miles to her apartment. One of the things she loved about Last Hope was how safe she felt here. She parked her car and started up the walkway toward her apartment, when she saw something in the shadows. Someone was on her porch. Her heart began to race, then the man looked up and she recognized him.

"Luke! What are you doing here?"

Chapter Nine

Luke stepped into the light. "I've been waiting for you."

Jenny tensed, both excited and angry. "Earlier, you couldn't seem to get away from me fast enough." She brushed past him and unlocked her door. The best thing to do was go into her apartment and leave him standing there.

"I shouldn't be here now, either," he said. "If I was smart, I'd leave you so fast—"

"Then why don't you?" she cut him off. "Just leave."

"Dammit, woman!" He grabbed her arm and leaned so close she could feel his breath on her face. "Don't you think I've tried? But you keep drawing me back. With your gorgeous brown eyes, those pouty lips that I've ached for since I pulled you out of the blizzard. Your shapely little body that keeps me aroused just thinking about you. Thinking about you in my bed. How much I want you." He backed her through the door. "Want you so bad I can't see straight." He reached behind and closed the door. Leaning against it, he jerked Jenny into the cradle of his open thighs and she gasped.

"Tell me I'm not alone," he begged. "Tell me you feel the same way."

Jenny could hear her pulse pounding in her ears as she let her purse slide to the floor. Then she placed her hands against his chest, feeling his erratic heartbeat. "Yes, Luke...I want you."

Luke groaned and covered her mouth with his. Parting her lips, his tongue eagerly invaded her warmth. The kiss was hot and hungry, and nearly out of control. He couldn't get enough.

He dragged his mouth from hers and began unbuttoning her blouse. Their breathing was rapid and labored. Finally, the material slid off her shoulders, and he worked the denim skirt down her hips. "I forgot to mention how nice you looked tonight." He knew he was acting like a teenager, but he couldn't seem to stop himself.

"You looked pretty good yourself," Jenny answered as she managed to strip off his shirt, then began planting soft kisses on his bare chest.

Damn! he wasn't going to survive. Luke swung Jenny up in his arms, and when she didn't protest, he carried her down the hall to her bedroom. The moonlight shone through the window, bathing the room in a soft glow. He brought her to the bed and gently placed her on the comforter. He followed her down, lying next to her. Reaching out, he unfastened the clasp on her bra, freeing her breasts into his hands. She pushed against his palm, eagerly offering herself to him. His mouth closed over the tip of one nipple, bring it to a taut peak. Hearing her moan, he continued the assault on the other.

Jenny nearly came off the bed when Luke's tongue touched her skin. The unbelievable pleasure had her gripping the comforter to keep herself from crying out.

He raised his head and whispered close to her mouth, "I meant what I said, Jenny. I want you. I want to make love to you."

"I want you, too." She gasped for air as he leaned over her, his bare chest moving against her, the abrasion causing an incredible sensation.

His mouth covered hers again, and again, while his hands moved expertly over her body, making her delirious with need.

"Oh, Luke." Her hands were caressing him, too. "I'm falling in love with you."

Jenny felt the change in Luke immediately. First, he froze, then he raised himself and looked down at her. The heated passion was gone. His eyes were cold and distant. She reached out with a trembling hand and he pulled away.

"Luke? What's wrong?" She refused to let him shut her out.

He sat up and turned his back to her. "Maybe we're making a mistake."

"What do you mean?" Jenny sat up, too, grabbing the edge of the comforter and covering herself. "I thought you wanted to make love? Did I do something?"

Luke shook his head. Hell, he was a coward. He didn't have the decency to face her. "I don't believe in love."

"Just because I said it... I didn't mean to make you feel that you had to say..."

He jerked around and took hold of her arms. "You should, Jenny. You deserve to hear the words." He hesitated. "I just can't say them."

Her large hopeful eyes raised to meet him. He could only watch as the tears formed.

"Maybe someday..."

He got off the bed. He had to put distance between them, or he'd forget all his good intentions. "No! I can't. I told you already I don't believe in love." He went to the window.

She followed him. "Why, Luke?" She touched her hand to his back and he nearly fell apart.

He flinched and swung around. "Because, Dammit! My wife destroyed all I had. All I have left are the memories of a wife who was never satisfied. I even tried to change to make her happy, but it didn't work. Cindy was bored with me, as a man, as a lover.... So she went out and found other men to hold her interest.'' He ignored Jenny's gasp. "I was relieved when she finally left town with another man. The real kicker was she wanted to take the kids.'' He clenched his hands, reliving the hellish nightmare. "I came unglued. But before we had a chance to fight it out in court, she was killed in a car accident.''

Luke drew a long breath and released it. His hungry gaze combed over Jenny's sweet face. "I'm all used up. There's no love left.''

She stood there for a long time, then finally said, "You know, Luke, I figured you to be stubborn, bullheaded and maybe even a little chauvinistic. But I never expected you to be a coward. I'm sure glad I found out before I...made a mistake.''

"Dammit, Jenny. I'm doing you a favor.''

"No you're not,'' she argued. "We could have had something wonderful, but you decided it isn't worth it. I'm not worth it. Well, I don't need you, Luke Reilly. There are plenty of men out there that think I'm worth taking a chance with.'' She pulled the blanket over her shoulders and walked to the bathroom, then paused and said over her shoulder, "Goodbye, Luke.''

It was after one in the morning when Luke walked through the double doors of the sheriff's office. The one-story brick building was quiet, as usual. He passed the glass-enclosed office and tossed a silent salute to the dispatcher, Johnny Allen, whose only job at present was finishing his dog-eared paperback. The other two deputies were on patrol, looking for hardened criminals in Last Hope.

At the end of the hall was the sheriff's office, where he found Tom sitting behind his desk, half glasses perched on his nose, going over paperwork.

Tom glanced up and smiled. "Well, look what the cat dragged in." He pulled off his glasses and stood up, giving his friend the once-over. "What brings you here?"

Luke dropped into the chair in front of the desk. "Heard you serve a pretty good cup of coffee."

Tom nodded, went and filled two mugs, then handed one to him. "How did the dance go?"

Luke raised an eyebrow. "You reporting to Molly?"

"Wouldn't make any difference if I was, she'll find out one way or the other."

Luke sighed. "I should have stayed home."

"That bad, huh?"

"I didn't belong there. It was Drew's territory."

"I figured you went to be with Jenny."

Luke studied his mug. "I had that crazy notion, too. I was mistaken."

"I take it she didn't have time for you."

Luke didn't answer. He closed his eyes and all he could see was the hurt look on Jenny's face. First at the dance...and later in her bedroom....

"That surprises me," Tom continued. "Every time I've seen her, she can't seem to take her eyes off you. I've also noticed that your reaction to her has been about as subtle as one of your bulls."

If you only knew, Luke thought, wanting to tell his friend the truth. Maybe then, Tom would stop trying to play matchmaker. Instead, he stood and moved across the room. "Things aren't what they seem. I don't have time for women."

"We're not talking about women, plural. We're talking about one special woman named Jenny Murdock."

Luke placed his mug down on the desk. "I can't do this again, Tom. Cindy destroyed anything I had left to give. She humiliated me—" Luke broke off. Tom had already heard the story. In fact, he'd been the only person that knew everything that had happened with his marriage. Even Molly didn't know all the sordid details.

"I know, son. Your wife did a royal job on you. I wanted to go after her myself." Tom didn't bother to hide his anger. "But dammit, you've got to allow yourself to forget the past and move ahead."

"How can I?"

"It's staring you in the face, boy. A good woman could change all that," Tom offered with a knowing grin. "All you have to do is give her a chance."

Somewhere deep inside, Luke ached to do just that, remembering how it felt to hold Jenny in his arms. How close he'd come to heaven. . . .

The entire weekend, Jenny had been a zombie. She'd cried nearly all night after Luke left. The rest of the weekend hadn't been much better. When she hadn't been crying, she'd been furious with him. She wanted to drive out to the ranch and give him a piece of her mind, and a couple of sucker punches in the midsection.

By Monday morning, she decided he wasn't worth it. But she knew deep in her heart that it didn't change how she truly felt. She was in love with Luke Reilly. But she had to get over it and get on with her life.

She walked into her office Monday morning and was greeted by an enthusiastic Ruth who wanted to talk about the dance.

"I thought everything went well. I can't believe all the men that showed up."

"We still need more women to come," Jenny reminded her, setting her briefcase on the desk. "I'm going to get more fliers out to the towns. I want to go as far out as Gillette."

"Boy, you're not messing around."

"It's my job," Jenny said.

"And your doing it well. How did your night go?"

"Not bad." Jenny looked away. "Several men asked me to dance."

"What about Luke?"

"What about him?"

"Oh, no. I take it the evening didn't go well for the two of you."

Jenny shook her head. "Do me a favor and don't ask for details. Or anything concerning Luke or Drew Reilly."

"Sure," Ruth agreed with a frown, then brightened. "Hey, who needs 'em? There are plenty of other men around."

Jenny burst out laughing and it felt good. "Yeah." But soon the tears started to form in her eyes. Darn it! She didn't want to cry anymore. "Who needs 'em?"

"When is the next dance?"

"Third Saturday in June," Jenny said. "Ruth, what do you think about having a hayride?"

The town clerk studied her for a moment. "All depends. If the right man snuggled up, it could be a lot of fun."

"Well, I've been thinking about holding one the weekend between the dance and the town's Fourth of July celebration. If couples want to spend more time together, it would be something to do rather than attend another dance."

"And another opportunity to find someone compatible," Ruth added as she studied Jenny closely. "Remember, there are plenty of men out there, especially for a pretty young thing like you."

Jenny nodded but didn't want to talk about men anymore. "Hey, you wouldn't happen to know where I can rent a team of horses and a wagon?"

Ruth pursed her lips. "I do, but you're not going to like it."

"Why? Won't he rent to us?"

"No. He'll rent. His father used to hire out for the annual fall harvest hayride given by the chamber of commerce years ago. Michael and Peg Reilly used to have everyone out to the ranch."

Jenny froze. "Luke's parents?"

Ruth nodded. "Let's see, back then, Luke was about five or six, and Drew couldn't have been more than a baby. Of course, that was for an all-day outing, kids included. In the evening, they'd load up the wagons with the adults and ride around the Double R Ranch, singing, telling stories. Or just cuddling up under the blankets." Ruth's sobered. "Then, after Peg died, they stopped having them."

"Maybe I should use another ranch."

"I bet Luke still has his dad's wagons."

The last thing Jenny wanted was to ask Luke for anything, not after...what had happened between them. "Well, I should at least see about other ranchers . . . just in case."

"Boy, you two really must have had a heck of a fight if you're willing to go to a stranger."

Jenny avoided Ruth's curious gaze. "I'd just prefer to check out the best prices."

"Well, there are several ranches around, but I'm not sure if they'd want to put on a hayride. I'll get you some phone numbers, though." Ruth started for the door, then paused. "I don't know what happened between you and Luke, and I figure it's none of my business. But he's a good man. And it might take him a little longer to learn to trust again."

Jenny bit down on her lip and nodded. Could she really work through the wall around his heart?

Ten days later, the next dance had come and gone. It had been even more crowded than the first, and there were also more women. Jenny had spent some time mingling and finding out what people wanted. There was a good response to the suggestion of a hayride.

Jenny had tried just about every rancher on Ruth's list, but most of them didn't want to mess with a hayride. It didn't matter to them that she would be doing all the work. And the ranchers who did agree were asking a fortune for a two-hour ride around their property. There was no choice. She had to ask Luke.

Of course, she could let Drew talk to his brother. But he seemed to be avoiding her lately. He hadn't even come to the dance over the weekend, using the excuse that he had to go out of town. He had called in every day, but it had been nearly a week since he'd come into the office.

Jenny knew she was good at her job, and happy that Drew felt he could leave her to run things. She did have some ideas she wanted to discuss with the mayor, so they could take them to the next town council meeting. There were also things to finalize for the big Fourth of July picnic.

Yes, she'd been busy. But at least her work had kept her from thinking about Luke.

Not really, but it is filling up my days and nights, Jenny thought as she unlocked the door to her apartment and walked inside the dark entry. She flicked on the light and dropped her purse on the table. Unable to stand it any longer, she kicked off her high heels on the way to the bedroom, then stripped out of her clothes and quickly put on a pair of jeans and a T-shirt. She dug into her closet for her comfortable, ratty-looking tennis shoes, wondering if she should call her mother tonight.

Caroline Murdock wasn't going to be happy when her daughter told her the news that she wasn't going to make it home for the Murdock Fourth of July barbecue. Jenny tied her shoelaces, knowing it was going to be impossible to spend a long weekend in Texas when she had work on Last Hope's own celebration.

Her mother would probably understand, but Ty... He would come unglued, spouting off about family loyalty and what would Dad say if...

Yeah, what would Dad say? Jenny wondered, remembering how close they had been over the years. J. T. Murdock had been the worst at spoiling his only daughter, but with love. Lots of love. So much so, Jenny had taken it for granted. Not anymore, she thought as her thoughts turned to Luke.

The phone rang and brought Jenny out of her reverie. Stretching across her bed, she picked it up. "Hello."

"Jenny, it's Luke."

Her heart pounded hard with optimism. "Hello, Luke."

"Jenny, I hate to bother you.... I tried to call Ms. Hart, Crissy's teacher, but she's not home. There's something wrong with Crissy."

Jenny sat up. "Is she hurt?"

"No, not physically, but she's been in her room all day, and she's crying a lot."

Jenny could hear the frustration in his voice. "Do you want me to come out?"

There was a long pause. "Yes, Jenny, I need you."

The words were like an aphrodisiac. "I'll be there in twenty minutes." She hung up, grabbed her purse and headed for the door.

Luke paced the floor as Garrett sat on the sofa. "Crissy is just crying to get attention."

Luke stopped. "Like you do?"

"I don't cry," his son denied, his bottom lip set in a pout.

"No, you don't." He leaned down and hugged Garrett. "But sometimes girls do, and I'm worried that there's something wrong. Crissy won't tell me."

"Is she real sick? Will she die?"

"No, Garrett. Crissy isn't going to die. But something is making her unhappy." He was, too, Luke thought as he got up and continued pacing.

"Is that why you called Jenny instead of the doctor?"

"Yeah, I think Crissy needs another girl to talk to."

"I like to talk to Jenny just because she makes me feel good." He nodded. "She'll make Crissy feel better."

Out of the mouths of babes. He knew firsthand how good Jenny could make a person feel. The touch of her hands, the feel of her body against his, the way—

The knock on the door drew his attention back to the present and he let Garrett hurry to answer it. He watched his son and Jenny exchange hugs. He tensed, knowing that his reception wasn't going to be as friendly. She finally glanced up and her beautiful smile disappeared.

"Hello, Luke."

"Thanks for coming," he said as he moved toward her. She stepped aside. "Is Crissy still in her room?"

"Yeah," he said bleakly. "She's been there most of the day." His starved gaze combed her face, then moved to her T-shirt and faded jeans.

"Then I'll go up and see if she wants to talk." Jenny walked toward the stairs as Luke watched the gentle sway of her hips. His body began to stir and he quickly glanced away.

"Hey, son. How 'bout a game of Go Fish?"

Luke spent the next forty-five minutes letting his son win at cards.

"Dad, how come Jenny doesn't come here anymore?" Garrett asked after a while.

Luke shrugged. "I guess she's been busy."

"Well, you like her, don't you?"

"Yeah."

"Then ask her to come."

He didn't know how to answer. God only knew that he wanted Jenny around, a lot. But it wasn't fair to ask her to be involved in a relationship that wasn't going anywhere. Besides, she could have any man in Last Hope, or in the county, for that matter. But Luke knew deep down, he didn't want another man in her life. And it sure as hell wasn't going to be Drew, if he could help it.

He looked up and saw Jenny come down the stairs. Luke tossed down his cards and got up.

"Did Crissy tell you what was wrong?"

Jenny started to speak, then glanced at Garrett. "Will you go and get me something to drink?" she asked the little boy.

"Sure." Garrett took off.

Jenny looked back at Luke. "Your daughter is fine. She's just going through some changes. Womanly changes."

Luke blinked in surprise. "You mean she . . . But she's only . . . She won't be twelve until next month." He rubbed his hand over his face.

"Whatever you do, don't make a big thing out of this. Right now, she's embarrassed about your even knowing. That's natural. I felt the same way."

Jenny started to leave.

"Wait. What am I supposed to do?"

She smiled. "Give her some space. Crissy's had to be sister, daughter and mother around here. It's a pretty rough job."

Luke knew that as content as he'd been to lead the single life, his kids had suffered. "Yeah, you're right."

"If it's okay with you, I said I'd take Crissy shopping. She wants something to wear for the Fourth of July picnic. Do you have a problem with that?"

"Of course not."

Jenny knew that Luke was in shock. His little girl was growing up. She was thrilled that he had asked for her help, but she wasn't naive enough to think that he wanted any more than just friendly womanly advice for his daughter.

"Maybe I can pick her up tomorrow afternoon, and she can spend the night with me."

Her gaze met his dark eyes and her pulse leaped. How she ached to be in his arms. Had he missed her as much as she had missed him. "I . . . I'd better be going."

He touched her arm to stop her. "Can't you stay?"

"Yeah, stay, Jenny." Garrett came in from the kitchen, carrying a glass of cola.

She took it from him. "Well, maybe for a little while. There's something I have to ask your father." She turned to Luke. "Would you be interested in having a hayride here on the Double R a week from Saturday?" She raised her hand to hold off his protest. "We'd be willing to pay you for the wagon and, of course, we want you to drive the team."

"The only way I'd agree to the whole thing would be if I drove."

"You mean, you'll do it?"

"Sure. I have a flatbed wagon that's in pretty good shape. And I'll check out a route and let you know."

"Thanks, Luke."

"No, thank you, Jenny."

She had to glance away, his dark eyes were too penetrating. "C'mon, Garrett. How about a few quick games of blackjack?" she offered.

"Oh, boy."

Luke folded his arms across his chest. "You're teaching my son to gamble?"

"No, Dad," Garrett said. "Jenny's teaching me math. So when I start school I'll be smart." The boy took off to get the cards.

They were left alone and Jenny's uneasiness grew. She walked toward the table in the dining room, and Luke followed her.

"Jenny, about what happened the other night," he began.

She shook her head. "Luke, it's okay." It took all the courage she could gather to look the man she loved in the eye and lie. "It's for the best."

The night of the hayride came around and Jenny was convinced that this wasn't the greatest idea she had come up with. The weatherman was predicting rain, and more men than women signed up for what Jenny had advertised as a romantic moonlit ride through the Wyoming countryside.

Luckily, Shelly and Ruth had come to Jenny's rescue and volunteered to go. Ruth also brought a female friend. Jenny hoped this was the last of her problems.

She arrived early, and by the looks of things, Luke had everything under control. The wagon was hitched up to a team of horses. In the corral, he had bales of hay arranged in a circle around a fire ring. She was impressed.

The tables were also set up with food. A barbecue was ready to start roasting hot dogs and hamburgers. Jenny had hired two men to help with the cooking and serving. Things under control, she went to look for Luke.

She caught him coming out of the house. And she could only stop and stare. He was dressed in new jeans, a starched, blue Western shirt and a pair of buckskin boots. He had his denim jacket, hooked on his finger, slung over his shoulder and his tan Stetson, resting low on his forehead.

Being from Texas, she'd seen a lot of cowboys, but none lived the image like this man.

Luke stopped in front of her and tipped his hat. "Good evenin', Jenny. Do I look okay?"

Oh, boy. How was she going to survive tonight? "Yes." She managed to find her voice. "In fact, everything looks great. The food, the wagon." Her hand swept the area. "It should be a great night."

"Well, that's what you hired me for."

"Yeah, that's what I hired you for," she murmured. "Do you think you can do anything about the weather?" As she spoke, the wind picked up, blowing her hair in her face. She brushed it away and pushed her hat farther down on her head.

"You can't let a little rain put a damper on your fun," Luke advised as two cars pulled into the driveway. "C'mon." He took her by the arm. "Let's go greet our guests."

Jenny tossed him a confused look, but walked with him to welcome the couples.

The next hour, an excited group of twenty-nine ate dinner. There were ten actual couples, four single women and five single men, including her and Luke. Nobody seemed to mind the odd number as they loaded the wagon with blankets and a cooler of soft drinks.

Shelly was sitting next to Matt Rider, a high school teacher from Last Hope. Ruth and her friend were near the end of the wagon, listening intently to two nice-looking elderly gentlemen. Jenny glanced around the wagon and everyone seemed to be getting along rather well.

As she turned on her portable tape player, she saw a streak of lightning flashing across the sky. It was far off, and no one else seemed to notice it. So, making sure everyone was secure in the wagon, she gave Luke the sign. He drove the team out of the corral and everyone cheered as they started their journey.

Soon, people were making conversation, and laughter broke out as voices raised to sing along with the music.

Jenny decided to climb up on the front bench and let everyone do their own thing for a while. She was going to enjoy herself. She studied Luke's hands as they worked the reins. Another flash of lightning.

"Do you think it's going to rain?" It was after eight, the sky was dark, but she could see the clouds moving overhead.

"It could, but then maybe not." She caught his smile.

"Well, maybe you'd better think of an escape plan if we get a sudden downpour."

"Don't worry, Ms. Murdock. I won't let your party get ruined."

All of a sudden, a big raindrop fell on Jenny's face, then another and another. "Well, you'd better come up with it," she said. "And quick." Over her shoulder, she saw everyone diving under the covers, trying to stay dry.

Luke gave a sharp whistle to the horses and they picked up their pace. In another few minutes, he pulled off the trail toward a grove of trees, and a ramshackle building came into view. Jenny didn't care, the rain was really coming down and she was nearly soaked by the time Luke drove the wagon inside the old barn.

He jumped down and immediately checked the horses, then came back to help people off the back, making sure they'd all survived. Jenny did the same. Everyone was fine, just a little cold and damp.

Luke lit two lanterns he'd brought along, then searched the area and found some dry wood. He'd had a feeling it was going to rain, but hadn't wanted to spoil Jenny's hayride. So he'd chosen the route closest to the old hay barn just in case. Some of the men helped him clear a spot near the door and he started a small campfire. Soon people gathered around the warmth and started singing. Everyone seemed to be having a good time once again.

Luke looked at Jenny and found her shivering in her wet clothes. She had been more concerned about everybody else to take the time to look after herself. That had been the one thing he'd discovered about her. She was always thinking of other people, before herself. Well, it was time that someone took care of her for a change. He reached under the seat of the wagon and pulled out a blanket.

He walked up behind her and draped it over her shoulders. "You need to get closer to the fire." He tried to nudge her, but she wouldn't budge.

"I'm fine." Her teeth were chattering.

"Like hell you are."

Jenny glanced around. "Please, Luke. I'm fine. I'm worried about everybody else. What if someone gets sick?"

"Jenny, every one of these people are old enough to come in out of the rain. And with help, they did." Suddenly, a roar of laughter filled the barn. "Besides, do they sound angry?"

Jenny shook her head and brushed back her wet hair. "I guess not." She looked up at him, her eyes big and bright. "Thank you, Luke. You helped so much." She started to go back to the group.

Luke couldn't let her leave. He grabbed her wrist and pulled her around to the front of the team. Ignoring the startled look on her face, he drew her against him and covered her inviting mouth with his. It was a long, needy kiss. One that he wanted to last forever. He wrapped his arms around her and used his body to warm her, but he got more. She responded, giving herself freely to the passion.

Finally, he pulled back, holding back a groan as he looked down at her wet and swollen mouth.

"You're welcome," he whispered.

Chapter Ten

"Will that leave you enough room for the booths and the tables?" Drew asked, leaning his elbows on the desk.

Jenny sat in the chair across from him, taking notes on the upcoming Fourth of July celebration. "It all depends on how many people show up for the picnic. Besides, we need the stage to make announcements...and speeches." She smiled. "Wouldn't want our mayor to get frustrated, unable to talk with his constituents."

Drew cocked an eyebrow. "This town's mayor better start worrying about his administrative assistant stealing his job."

Jenny's mouth dropped open. "I don't want your job."

"Yeah, but with your sudden popularity in the matchmaking department, you'd probably beat me without much effort."

"All I did was organize a few socials."

"No, that's not quite true," he disagreed. "You went and found out what people wanted." He opened a file on his desk. "I've been going over some of your other ideas. With everything else you've been doing, how did you find the time to think up things like mixed-doubles bowling nights, switching to different teams every week?"

"That's so you get a chance to meet more people," she offered.

"Country line-dance classes during the day for exercise and at night for socializing." Drew raised an eyebrow.

"It's a great aerobic exercise," she volunteered, wondering if she'd gone too far. She'd needed to keep busy the past few weeks.

"I want to hear more about this day-care center." He waved his hand. "But after we survive the picnic on Sunday."

Jenny smiled and nodded. When Drew had come back to town, they'd had a long talk. She'd made him understand how she felt and how much she wanted to be his friend and continue to work for him. Drew told her he wished things could be different between them, but that he never wanted to lose her friendship.

They'd also talked about his problem relationship with Luke and the fate of the Double R. Although Drew never said anything, she'd had a suspicion that his being out of town the past week had more to do with the ranch's mineral rights than with town business. But if something wasn't settled soon between the brothers, she thought, they might lose more than just the ranch.

"How about we stop for some lunch?" he suggested.

"Sounds good," she agreed. "I need to talk to Molly, anyway, about some pies for the picnic."

Jenny stood just as there was a rapping sound on the door. She answered it to find her brother standing on the other side.

"Brett!" she cried and jumped into his arms.

Brett responded by picking up his sister and swinging her around in a big hug.

"I'm so glad to see you," she said when he finally set her.

He grinned, showing off his straight pearly-white teeth. "Good. I had business in Gillette. I thought I'd stop by to see how you're doing." He glanced around the office, then at Drew.

"Oh, I'm sorry," Jenny apologized as she took her brother by the arm. "Drew, this is my brother, Brett. Brett, I'd like you to meet Drew Reilly, the mayor of Last Hope, and my boss."

"Yeah, sure. Like someone could boss you." He offered his hand to the mayor. "Nice to meet you, Drew. I hope I'm not interrupting anything."

Drew shook Brett's hand. "It's nice to meet some of Jenny's family. And no, we were just going to take a break. So your sister can show you a little of our town and take you to lunch."

Jenny glanced at Drew and mouthed a silent thank-you. "I promise I'll be back in an hour." She pulled Brett out the door and toward her office. She quickly showed him around, then grabbed her purse when the phone rang.

Jenny picked it up. "Hello, Jenny Murdock."

"Jenny, it's Molly."

"Oh, Molly, I was just coming over for lunch. I've got someone I want you to meet."

"Well, I'm not at the restaurant, I'm at Hope Clinic."

Jenny's smile vanished. "Is something wrong?"

"Luke brought Garrett in. He fell out of the loft."

"Oh, my God. How bad is he hurt?"

"I don't know. I just thought you should come by." There was a long sigh. "There are two guys here that look like they need you."

"I'll be right there."

Jenny rushed through the door of the small clinic, Brett close on her heels. She went to the desk and asked the receptionist, "Is there a Garrett Reilly here?"

"Yes, the doctor is examining him now."

Before Jenny could ask anything more, she heard her name called out. She turned and found Molly coming across the waiting room.

"How's Garrett?" Jenny asked anxiously.

"He's fine. He's got a couple of bruises, two stitches over his eyes and a sprained arm," she explained as she glanced at Brett. "And if I know that boy, he'll probably milk this for more Power Rangers, but I bet all that child's going to get is a wave of punishment from his father for putting him through this. Who's your friend?"

"I'm sorry, Molly. This is my brother Brett. Brett, Molly Willis. Can I see him?" Jenny found she couldn't just sit and wait.

"Hello, Brett," Molly said and Brett nodded. "I guess your sister isn't going to relax until she can see the patient for herself." Molly took Jenny to the desk and told the nurse that she was a relative.

Leaving Brett in Molly's capable hands, Jenny followed the nurse down the long corridor.

Suddenly, Jenny flashed back to seven years ago when her niece, Becky, had been in a car accident. The four-year-old was in a coma for nearly a month. A chill rushed down Jenny's back and she absently rubbed her arms.

The nurse finally stopped at the doorway and motioned for her to go in. Heart in her throat, Jenny peered into the examining room and saw Garrett sitting on the table. The nurse was adjusting a white sling, cradling his small arm. There was a big bandage over his left eye and a long ugly scrape along his once flawless cheek.

Jenny glanced at Luke, who was talking with the doctor. Worry lines creased his forehead. She wished he would let her share his pain. She stepped into the room.

"Boy, what some people won't do for attention."

Garrett looked at her and his face lit up. "Jenny!" he cried and immediately tears filled his eyes. "I got hurt."

She rushed to him and took him in her arms, careful not to hurt his injuries. "I know, sweetheart. Molly told me you fell out of the loft."

"I was on the ladder. Dad said I shouldn't have been there." The child's lower lip trembled. "He's mad at me."

Jenny leaned over. "I think your daddy was just scared because you hurt yourself."

"But I did a bad thing. I'm not supposed to be on the ladder."

Jenny fought against the tears threatening. "But you're okay. And that's the most important thing." She kissed the end of his freckled nose. "Ooooh, you scraped your cute little face."

A tear ran down his cheek. "Do you still like me, Jenny? Even though I did a dumb thing?"

She swallowed hard and looked up at Luke. "Garrett, there's nothing you could do to ever make me stop liking you. No matter what. Just promise me, you'll stay out of lofts."

The boy nodded and hugged her. "I promise."

Luke walked out of the room. His emotions were too raw to handle seeing Jenny. Even if he had to admit to himself that he was never so happy as when he'd seen her come through the door. He rubbed his forehead, remembering how he'd nearly come apart when he found Garrett lying on the barn floor.

"You've had a rough day."

He turned, hearing Jenny's soft voice.

She looked like an angel, with her fresh-scrubbed face and her hair all soft and curly. She was wearing a red skirt and matching jacket. Black heels still made her short compared to his height. But he knew all too well that she was the perfect size for him.

"I've had better."

She smiled. "Well, the good thing is, Garrett wasn't seriously hurt."

"Hell, he could have been." Luke wasn't fooling himself about the seriousness of today's incident. "I only took my eye off him for a few minutes."

Jenny touched his arm. "C'mon, Luke. Kids are like that. They're into everything, wanting to discover the world."

He looked down at her small hand resting on his forearm. "I could have lost him...." Luke was tired. He was tired of doing it all alone.

"Where was Crissy?"

"She stayed overnight at a friend's house."

"Maybe it's time to look for a housekeeper again."

"You know I've tried. The results haven't been great."

"Would you mind if I did some checking around?"

Luke studied her for a moment. "No, I wouldn't."

She smiled, and his pulse went soaring. "Good." She started to walk away, but Luke stopped her.

"Thanks, Jenny. I know I have no right to ask you to help, but you always seem to be there...for the kids."

"Why are you so surprised, Luke?" she said with a frown. "Not everyone is like Cindy."

He met her accusing gaze. "I know it's a little late, but I'm beginning to realize that."

Her expression softened. "I guess that's something."

Luke wanted desperately to reach out to her. "But not enough."

Jenny bit down on her lower lip. He could see she was fighting back her tears. "It wouldn't be enough for either one of us."

He wanted to argue the point, when someone called Jenny. They both looked up and saw a tall man coming down the hall.

"Jenny, is everything okay?" the man asked.

"It's fine, Brett. Garrett's fine." She looked back at Luke, seeing his confusion. "Brett, this is Garrett's father, Luke Reilly. Luke, this is my brother, Brett Murdock."

The two men sized each other up, then Brett offered his hand and said, "Reilly, I'm glad everything turned out okay."

Luke shook it. "Thanks." He eyed Jenny's dark-haired brother, seeing a family resemblance. "You came all this way to see Jenny?"

"Actually, I'm here on business, in Gillette." Brett laid his arm across her shoulders. "I just came down to bug Jenny. Find out if she's come up with any prospects for a husband."

Luke tensed as Jenny smacked her brother playfully. But there was nothing playful about the idea. Jenny was a beautiful woman. Any man would be lucky to have her. "I'm not sure about that. She's been busy matchmaking for nearly everyone else in town."

Luke's eyes met Jenny's and they exchanged a heated gaze. He couldn't deny he wanted her. But he'd never have her, so he'd better get used to it.

It was only eight o'clock and already the sky was clear, the sun bright, and the temperature was predicted to hit a comfortable seventy-five degrees. It was turning out to be a lovely day for a picnic, better than Jenny had hoped.

Dressed in old jeans and a T-shirt, Jenny helped supervise the placement of the tables, making sure everyone had enough room. The stage went up behind the fountain, which was going to be rededicated today. There were red, white and blue banners strung throughout the town. Every shop had colorful plants and awnings to enhance the completed refacing project. She glanced around the town square. It looked perfect.

She turned and found Molly and Tom coming toward her. "Jenny, it all looks wonderful," Molly said, beaming.

"I know. Isn't it great?" Jenny said, then turned to Tom. "Tom, what about parking? Did Harry Doyle agree to let us use the lot behind his store?"

"With a little persuading," Tom began. "I had to remind him about the illegal parking I've overlooked through the years."

"Good." Molly nodded. "That old buzzard needs to be a little more charitable. And the Fourth of July is a great time to bring the community together."

"Well, this was all Drew's idea, but it's a lot bigger than expected." Jenny turned around and watched as the booths were being set up. "It seems that every organization wanted space."

"That just adds to the fun," Molly confirmed. "I can't wait until the picnic-basket auction."

Jenny focused on her friend. "I'm not sure about that. Did you get enough participants?"

Molly's eyes rounded. "Are you kidding? Several women have ordered my fried chicken and apple pie."

Tom grinned. "That's false advertising, if you ask me."

Molly poked him in the ribs. "Hey, whatever it takes to get a man to the altar. Are you going to put in a basket, Jenny?"

"Oh, no, I'll be too busy with the activities."

"You should never be too busy for romance."

Jenny watched the loving look exchanged between the couple. "Maybe next year." She saw one of the crew waving at her. "I'd better get back to work. See you later." She walked off, praying that she was going to make it through the day. Maybe she should have gone back to Texas for the family barbecue. At least she wouldn't feel so alone.

Two hours later, Jenny arrived dressed in a new red and white sundress. She was wearing comfortable sandals, and her hair was pulled back with combs and hung over her shoulders. She'd decided to forget about makeup and let the sun give her color. She cheated with a little lip gloss, which she would have chewed off before lunch, anyway.

Right at ten, she met Drew at the stage in front of the fountain. He, too, was dressed casually in a pair of tan chinos and a navy polo shirt. He was handsome, all right, and there was no doubt that the single women in the audience were interested in him, and not for his political views, either. She was happy that over the past weeks she and Drew had become a good working team as well as good friends.

Jenny released a long sigh. If only she had as satisfying a personal life. She surveyed the crowd in the town square hoping to find Luke, but so far she hadn't seen him. She hoped nothing was wrong, remembering that Garrett was still recovering from his accident.

A round of applause caught her attention as for the first time in thirty years water spouted from the fountain.

The school band began to play "The Star-Spangled Banner," and Jenny was suddenly teary-eyed. She truly felt a part of this community. Everyone in Last Hope had been so welcoming and accepting.

Hearing her name, she turned toward the back of the stage and found Luke. He tossed her a wave and a grin. A warm shiver slid down her spine. Somehow, she managed to return the smile, but not without wondering if the ache she felt for this stubborn cowboy would ever go away. Or would she always be comparing him with every man that came into her life?

After the ceremony was concluded, Jenny stepped down from the stage and was greeted by Crissy. The blond girl was dressed in the outfit they'd picked out shopping together. The bright pink cotton top looked cute under a pair of bib overall shorts.

"Jenny, these are my friends." Crissy introduced three eleven-year-olds. Then Garrett came up to her. Wearing his sling like a badge of honor, he gave her a big hug.

"How are you feeling?" she asked the little boy.

"It doesn't hurt anymore," Garrett said, proudly showing her the pink scar over his eye. "I got my stitches out yesterday."

"I can see that." She stood up and came face-to-face with Luke. Her breath caught as the musky fragrance of his after-shave teased her nose.

Luke placed his hands on his son's shoulders. "Hello, Jenny. How have you been?"

She had trouble not staring. He was so handsome. "Busy."

"You've done a great job."

She felt tongue-tied. "Well, I had a lot of help."

Luke arched an eyebrow. "Drew?"

"Of course Drew. He's the mayor, and I also had a committee." Jenny was grateful when one of her volunteers waved to get her attention. "Looks like I better get back to work."

Luke stopped her departure and asked, "Do you think you could have lunch with us?"

"I'm sorry. I probably won't have time."

Luke glanced away, but not before she caught his hurt look. "Sure, I understand," he said.

Well, she didn't. From the moment she'd met Luke Reilly, she never knew what to expect from the man. She looked down at Garrett. "Maybe I'll see you later."

"Okay," the boy agreed.

By noon, the celebration was in full swing, and Jenny was ready for a break. Not that she could take one, she thought as she walked passed the carnival booths lining Main Street. There was a dunk tank sponsored by the high school, another popular attraction was a dime toss, and of course the ring toss kept the little kids busy.

She made her way toward the stage area where they were starting the picnic-basket auction. It had drawn quite a crowd. Molly and Tom Willis were at the microphone, holding up the first basket. The bidding started at five dollars, and all proceeds were to go into the building fund for the new community center.

At first, the men seemed shy, but Tom got it going by practically drooling over the contents of Mary Jane Kelly's basket. One of the men bid twenty dollars, and the offers quickly escalated to thirty-five. After the gentleman paid Molly, he took the basket and Mary Jane, and they went off to find a spot for a picnic.

Molly reached for another basket. "This here basket is filled with some wonderful fried chicken, potato salad, homemade rolls with real butter...and apple pie for dessert. And the basket also comes attached to the very pretty Jenny Murdock.''

The crowd cheered and Jenny felt the blood rush to her face. She hadn't entered the auction. When did she have time to cook, anyway? She glared at a smiling Molly.

"What am I bid for the basket and lunch with a lovely lady?"

The bids started at twenty, but quickly worked up to forty dollars. "C'mon, men," Tom began, "our Jenny is worth far more than forty dollars. She's worked hard on this picnic today. It's time we show her that we appreciate her."

Another man's hand went up. "Forty-five."

"Forty-five going once, going twice . . ."

"One hundred dollars!" a voice called out and everyone gasped. Jenny did, too. She raised onto her toes and searched the crowd to find that Luke had made the bid. Her heart leaped for joy.

Tom's smile widened. "Well, now, that's what I call a fair bid. Now, is there anyone else who wants to . . . challenge?" The sheriff glanced around, looking satisfied that no one took him up on the offer. "Looks like she's all yours, Luke."

The crowd grew silent as Luke walked to the stage. He pulled out the money and handed it to Tom. Then he took the basket and stepped off the stage. Jenny's heart began to race as Luke's slow, purposeful gait caused the crowd to separate, leaving a clear path directly to her.

He tipped his hat back. "I believe you just found time for lunch."

All she could do was nod as he took her hand and they started off together. "Wait, what about the kids?" she asked.

"Don't worry, they'll be taken care of," he told her.

Luke borrowed a blanket, then they made their way to the other side of the park, away from everyone at the picnic. He spread the blanket on the grass next to the creek, and made a sweeping motion with his hand as he offered her a seat. Slowly, Jenny dropped to her knees and Luke followed her.

"Look," she began, "before we start, I want you to know that I didn't make anything in that basket. It's probably Molly's."

"I know. It was my idea to put your name on the basket."

Jenny's heart was racing like crazy. "Why?"

His eyes were dark and searching, his voice husky. "Because I wanted to be with you."

"Oh, Luke," she breathed. "I don't think this is such a good idea. . . ."

He shook his head. "It's the best idea I've had in a long time." The basket was forgotten as he reached out and cupped the back of her neck, then lowered his mouth over hers.

Jenny released a frustrated moan and pushed against his chest. A tear ran down her cheek and she pulled away. "No, Luke, please. Don't do this to me."

He touched her chin, making her look at him. "Please, Jenny, don't cry. I don't want to make you unhappy anymore. I just can't stay away. You're in my head all day. At night when I try to sleep. Damn! I ache for you all the time. . . ." He closed his eyes and drew a long breath. "I was wrong about us. I need you in my life. We all need you, Crissy and Garrett, too." He swallowed. "Marry me, Jenny."

Jenny's heart was lodged somewhere between her chest and her throat. Luke wanted to marry her. "Luke, we can't—"

"Why?"

She opened her mouth, but no words came out. She finally pulled away from his hold and stood. "The fact that you don't love me seems like a good reason."

She studied Luke for what seemed like forever, praying that he would deny it. He didn't.

Luke got to his feet, but she knew from his expression that he couldn't give her the words she wanted to hear.

"There are lots of reasons people get married, Jenny," he said. "I want to take care of you." His arms slipped around her waist and pulled her against him. "And I've never wanted a woman as much as I want you. You're the right one for me."

Jenny felt herself tremble.

"We could make a good life . . . you and me . . . the kids." He leaned down and nibbled her neck. "I'll do everything possible to make you happy. I may not be rich, but you'll never want for anything. I have plans for the future. Our future."

This wasn't what she had envisioned as a proposal. But she loved this man, more than she ever imagined possible. Most important, she wanted to help him find that trust he'd lost long ago. It might take time, but she vowed Luke Reilly would discover love again.

"Yes," she whispered.

He stared, complete surprise on his face. "What?"

"I said yes. I'll marry you."

Chapter Eleven

"Like hell you're getting married," Tyler Murdock bellowed into the receiver. "If I have to come up there—"

"Ty, you have no right to tell me what to do." Jenny's voice lowered as she turned away from the kitchen table where Luke and the children were seated.

"And you have no right to marry this Reilly guy when you've only known him for such a short time."

"I've known him as long as you knew Maggie before you got married," she countered. "Three months. And if you want to give your sister away, I suggest you behave yourself. The wedding is planned for the middle of August." Jenny bit her lip. Was she doing the right thing? She looked at Luke sitting at the table with Crissy and Garrett. How she loved them. There was no way she could be making a mistake. "Please, Ty, just be happy for me. I want all the family here."

There was a long pause. "Ah, hell, you always did have me wrapped around your finger." He sighed. "Do I have to wear a stupid monkey suit?"

She had him. "I don't care if you wear jeans and your favorite old Stetson. I just want you to give me away."

"Don't think we're not coming early to check this guy out."

"Good. Well, I'd better go. Tell Mom I love her, and I'll call her tomorrow after work." She hung up, drew a long breath and released it.

"I take it your family wasn't too happy over the announcement," Luke said.

"Surprised is a better word." Jenny went to the table. "But they don't know you." She smiled at Garrett and Crissy. "When my mother meets you two, she's gonna love you both."

"Will she be our grandmother?" Garrett asked, and Crissy poked him in the ribs. "I was only asking a question."

"It's a good question, too." Jenny smiled. "Yeah, I guess she will be."

"What do we call her?"

"Whatever you want. Her name is Caroline. Then there's your uncle Tyler, who looks mean but loves kids. His wife is Maggie, and they have three kids, Becky, Zach and little J.W. My other brother, Brett, is married to Jessie. They don't have any kids yet, but Jessie has two brothers, Mac and Josh, and a sister, Katie. A big family, huh?"

Both children nodded, then Garrett looked up at her with his brown eyes and asked. "What are we supposed to call you, Jenny?"

How had the month flown by? Jenny wondered as she sat staring out the window in her office. Between wedding plans and her job, and trying to spend time with her soon-to-be family, Jenny was exhausted. Her mother had flown up once to Last Hope, and on another trip they'd met in Casper to shop for a dress. Caroline had been disappointed that there hadn't been enough time to special order, but Jenny had assured her that the bridal gown they found was perfect. She cared more about how her mother felt about Luke. Caroline admitted she liked him very much. Crissy and Garrett hadn't had much trouble winning over their future grandmother, either.

All Jenny wanted was to be done with the wedding. To be Mrs. Luke Reilly right now, living at the ranch, and the best part, sleeping in Luke's bed every night. Her cheeks grew warm, remembering stolen moments with her future husband, and how close they'd come to making love. But Luke had always stopped, promising her they'd wait until they were married.

One more week, Luke Reilly, and you're all mine.

Luke stood at the door, watching his future bride. Just the sight of her made his body stir with desire. This week was going to be the longest in his life, but he'd never been happier.

That was, until he'd come into town and asked Drew to be his best man. His brother had started spouting off about the damn survey again. If he hadn't promised Jenny not to start any arguments, he would have walked out. Instead, he'd agreed to a meeting after he and Jenny returned from their honeymoon.

Now, he had to find a way to keep the other promise to Jenny, and not touch her until their wedding night.

"Hey, you better be daydreaming about me," Luke said, and she turned around.

"Who else?" she said with a smile.

"Anything you want to tell me about?" He walked into her office and sat down on the edge of her desk.

Jenny stood and wrapped her arms around his neck. "Not such a good idea." Her voice lowered to a whisper. "What I'm thinking about isn't going to help our situation at all." She placed a kiss on the side of his neck. He groaned.

"Did you ask Drew to be your best man?" She continued her assault with her mouth.

"Yes, and he said he'd be honored. Stop that, woman, or I won't be held accountable for what happens."

She raised her head and smiled. "Oh, I like it when you talk like that." She snuggled against him.

"You keep this up and you'll get more than just talk."

Saturday morning, the First Calvary Church was completely decorated in pink and white roses. Satin bows had been tied to the front pews and a long, white runner covered the center aisle in preparation for Last Hope's biggest social event in years. The Murdock-Reilly wedding.

Jenny wasn't so sure she would be ready for the eleven-o'clock service. Her nerves still hadn't settled down since the arrival of her family two days ago. Between the last-minute things to do and her brothers' determination to get to know Luke better, she hadn't had a moment's peace.

Finally, last night, her sisters-in-law, Jessie and Maggie, along with Shelly, Ruth and Molly had thrown her a surprise bridal shower, while Tom Willis and Drew, Tyler and Brett, had taken the groom out to the local tavern for a wild evening on the town. Jenny's concern was that her brothers would interrogate Luke to death and he would decide she wasn't worth the effort. Would he leave her standing at the altar?

He'd better not, she thought as she eyed herself in the long mirror. The off-the-shoulder white gown had a fitted alençon lace bodice that dipped into a vee, accenting her small waist. The gathered skirt was silk chiffon that nearly touched the floor, angling into a long train behind her. The long sleeves were tapered into a delicate point at her wrist. Her floral headpiece was a halo of roses and baby's breath, woven through her hair and accented by an elbow-length veil.

"You look beautiful," Tyler said as he came into the room.

Jenny turned around. "I bet you say that to all the brides."

He shook his head. "Only to Maggie, and now you."

Ty was dressed in a gray morning coat with a pair of pin-striped trousers. His usually unruly sandy-colored hair was neatly trimmed. All her life she had looked up to this man. He'd been her hero. It meant the world to her that he was going to give her away.

"You remind me of Caroline."

"Mom?" Jenny was thrilled as she glanced back in the mirror. "I guess I do look pretty good for a tomboy."

Tyler shrugged. "I guess you couldn't help that. You had two brothers to keep up with."

"I think Dad made sure you let me win a few."

"All Dad said was not to let you get hurt," Tyler admitted.

She walked to him. "Maybe you were too protective."

"You were my only sister, Jen. What was I supposed to do?" He glanced away. "Okay, maybe when J.T. died, I went a little overboard...."

"Boy, this is quite a day. I'm marrying the man of my dreams, and my big brother admits he was wrong." She hugged him. "Oh, Ty, I know you did your best, and you were only trying to protect me. And honestly, I always liked having you there."

He touched her cheek. "Now you're going to replace me with another man." He released a long sigh. "But I have to admit, this Reilly guy doesn't seem too bad."

She blinked back tears. "Your saying that means a lot to me."

Brett peeked into the dressing room. "If you two are finished with all the sentimentality, the photographer would like to take a few pictures." Behind Brett, Maggie and Jessie followed, dressed in their rose-colored bridesmaid's dresses. Then Caroline appeared, wearing a teal-green suit. Her brown hair was worn short with diamond earrings adorning her ears. There was evidence of tears in her eyes as she went to her daughter.

"You look beautiful. Your daddy..." The words died off as both mother and daughter fought for composure. "He loved you so much."

Jenny nodded as she gripped her mother's hands. "I loved him, too. I miss him."

"He's with us, Jenny." Caroline touched her chest. "In here. When you walk down that aisle in a few minutes, just know that your father and I are giving you away to Luke with our blessing."

Luke heard the church bell chime just as the music began. Crissy started down the aisle as the first bridesmaid, then came Maggie Murdock, Garrett carrying the rings and finally Jessie Murdock appeared as the maid of honor. He wasn't sure of all their titles, only that he wanted the ceremony over and done with. Luke tugged at his collar and glanced at his calm-looking brother. Of course, he could act cool, Drew wasn't the one getting married, Luke thought as sweat beaded along his upper lip. He was beginning to wonder what he was doing here. Nervously, he searched the crowded church and found the Willises seated in the front row, Molly crying and Tom grinning.

The music changed and Jenny came into view at the back of the church. Even from a distance, her beauty radiated to where he stood at the altar. He watched as her brother, Tyler, took her hand and placed it on his arm and they started down the aisle. Luke's throat tightened as she walked toward him; not once did her gaze waver from his. When his bride took his hand at the altar step, she gave him a bright smile. Her brown eyes were aglow with tenderness and love.

You're one lucky man, Luke Reilly.

"To the bride and groom," Tyler began. "May your life together be filled with love and laughter."

Jenny's eyes were tearing as she listened to her family's wedding toasts. Even the best man was sincere and loving. She looked at her new husband seated next to her at the reception table. He didn't look as if he was enjoying himself.

"Luke, are you okay?"

He frowned. "When can we get out of here?"

"I think it's customary for the bride and groom to hang around to cut the cake."

"How long before we do that?"

"What's your hurry?"

He tossed her one of his sexy grins. "I'm just anxious to have my bride all to myself."

She reached for his hand. "And I'm anxious to be alone with my husband, too. But my family will be leaving after the wedding and…it will be a while before I get to see them again." Jenny saw the disappointment on his face. "Just think, your mother-in-law is going to be living hundreds of miles away."

"I think my mother-in-law is great. It's your brothers I'm not going to miss much."

"Oh, Brett and Tyler are harmless."

Before Luke could protest, they called the bridal couple to the dance floor. Jenny went into her new husband's arms as the guests cheered.

Caroline Murdock was the first to cut in during the bridal dance. She took Luke as a partner and Drew went to Jenny.

"I want you to know, Mrs. Murdock, that I'm going to do everything to make your daughter happy."

Caroline raised her chin in much the same way her daughter did. "I have no doubt you will, Luke," she began. "But Jenny is a Murdock." She smiled. "Believe me, you're going to have your hands full."

Drew swept Jenny around the dance floor with a flourish. She was beginning to wonder if Luke's brother did anything without looking for an audience.

"I can't tell you how happy I am that you're in the family. You're going to be so good for Luke."

"Luke's going to be good for me, too," Jenny added.

He looked thoughtful. "Now that you two are married...maybe you'll be able to talk some sense into my brother. I mean, about the survey."

Jenny didn't want to deal with this on her wedding day. "Drew, you know I don't want to be involved."

"As his wife, you are involved, Jenny. Besides, we already have a court date set for next month."

She stopped dancing. "When?"

"The fifteenth of September. Luke's already gotten one extension. So he can't put it off any longer."

Jenny wasn't listening anymore, she was too busy wondering why Luke hadn't told her about the hearing.

"My lawyer said the judge will likely divide the ranch and allow the testing. I'm not being unreasonable. I only want a couple of sections for the survey."

"Drew, how can you do this to your brother?"

"Look, Jenny, I'm entitled to what's mine."

"C'mon, Drew. You knew how your father felt."

He glanced away. "That was a long time ago. It's time for Luke to share the ranch. There's room for both of us. You can help, Jenny. Talk to your brother. If not, we'll be in court next month."

It wasn't fair. Today was her wedding day, there weren't supposed to be any problems. "Okay, I'll talk to Brett."

Jenny found her brother. "I need to talk to you."

"What's up, sis? Discovered you've made a mistake and want me to help you escape?"

"Close. Remember what I told you about Luke and Drew's problems over the ranch? Well, there's more. Drew's taking Luke to court next month over the mineral rights."

"What can I do?"

"Do you have time to do some preliminary studies on the Double R?"

Brett frowned. "Did Luke agree to this?"

She sighed. "Luke could end up losing the ranch with his stubbornness. I know you did some checking on the historical data in the Powder River Basin while you were in Gillette."

"They were just preliminary tests."

"Do you think there is anything worth looking into?"

"Could be."

"Could you be a little more thorough before you go back home?"

"Yeah, I can."

She hugged her brother. "Oh, thanks, Brett."

"Don't be thanking me, Jen. You might not like the results."

Jenny had no idea where Luke was taking her on their honeymoon. They only had five days, and planned not to go too far. With Crissy and Garrett waiting at home with Shelly Hart and the fall roundup in another month, they decided five days was about all they could take now.

When Luke pulled off the road at the back of the ranch, Jenny was surprised and intrigued, especially when he parked the Bronco in front of a small rustic cabin. She glanced around the isolated area and at the tall pines and small stream.

Luke turned in his seat. "I know it's not much," he began. "And if you'd rather, we could drive up to Gillette and spend a couple nights in a hotel."

"Don't you even think about it. I love it." She reached across the cab and kissed him. By the time he broke it off, they were breathless.

"I think we'd be more comfortable inside." He opened his door and got out, rushed around to the other side and pulled Jenny out into his arms. She giggled as he carried her up the rickety steps and kissed her again at the cabin door.

"I meant what I said about it being crude, Jen," he warned. "Outside of running water, there aren't too many luxuries."

She loved this man. "It's got you and me, and all the privacy in the world. What more could we want?"

"Oh, Jenny Reilly, what did I ever do to deserve you?"

She batted her eyes. "Nothing yet, Mr. Reilly, but I was hoping you'd remedy that real soon."

Luke groaned. "Be careful what you wish for. You may get more than you can handle," he teased as he reached down, turned the knob and pushed open the door.

With his beautiful bride in his arms, Luke stepped across the threshold. He kissed Jenny again, then set her down and hurried around the one-room cabin to light the kerosene lamps. When he finished, he looked at Jenny. She was busy taking in her surroundings. There was a stone fireplace, and a braided rug on the rough-planked floor. A worn sofa and a rocking chair made up the small sitting area. The scarred kitchen table was covered by a red-checked tablecloth. There was a big bouquet of flowers sitting next to an ice bucket that contained a bottle of wine and two glasses.

Jenny picked up the card. "It's from my family. 'To Mr. And Mrs. Reilly. Start your life together with a promise and love, no matter how rough the road may get. Always remember the love you shared on this your special day.'" Jenny glanced up at Luke and smiled. "It's signed, Mom and Dad."

"Tom must have brought it here. He and Molly are the only ones who knew we were coming to the cabin." Luke went to the table, took the bottle from the bucket and began opening it. "I think your parents have the right idea." He worked the corkscrew.

"Mom and Dad shared a wonderful marriage. I never saw two people more in love." Jenny moved around the small kitchen. She peeked into the old refrigerator, eyeing the food that he'd bought.

"I have a small generator out back so we can have hot water and cold food."

"Looks like you've thought of everything."

"I tried, but we can always make a run into town."

Jenny swung around. "Don't even think about it. As far as I'm concerned, this is paradise. You're going to have a lot of trouble getting me to leave on Friday." She continued her travels to the alcove, where a bridal ring-patterned quilt covered a new queen-size bed.

Luke walked up behind his wife. "This was Molly's idea, the flowers and the quilt. She also helped with the cleaning and the food. She said it was their wedding present to us."

Jenny leaned against him. "It couldn't be more perfect. I just hope we can come back sometime."

Luke pulled her tighter into his embrace. "We can. This cabin is on the ranch. Of course, it's been used as a hunting cabin more than a romantic getaway."

Jenny turned in his arms and placed her hands against his chest. "Well, Mr. Reilly, I guess I'll have to come out here sometime for lunch."

"I'll never get any work done." He bent his head and took her mouth in a hungry kiss. Pulling her against him, he let her know of his need. He'd never wanted a woman so much.

"Oh, Jenny, I want you so much," he breathed as he tore his mouth away from hers.

"Then what are we waiting for?"

Jenny walked out of the tiny bathroom dressed in her white satin gown and found Luke standing next to the bed. He was bare-chested, wearing only a pair of dark pajama bottoms. Damn! The man was sexy.

"I thought you were the most beautiful bride I had ever seen today, but now… You're like a dream." He offered her a glass of wine.

Jenny stepped closer. "No, Luke, I'm a woman. A woman who wants her husband very much." She reached up on her toes and kissed him, then took the flute from his hand.

"And I want you so much," he confessed. "I think I'm going to die from it. But I want to make it special for you."

"Just make love to me, Luke."

"First things first." He raised his glass and Jenny followed. "To us. To what we have together. I promise, Jenny, to always try and make you happy."

"And I promise to make you happy." She touched her crystal glass to his. Then they took a sip and placed the glasses on the table next to the bed.

Luke pulled the quilt back, exposing silk ivory sheets. Then he took his bride in his arm and kissed her, a long heated kiss. His tongue swept her mouth, hungry for her sweet taste, but knowing he'd never get enough.

Finally, he pulled his mouth away from hers and began nibbling on her neck, until he reached her shoulder, then tugged at the thin strap of her gown, letting it drop to expose her creamy skin. He closed his eyes and inhaled her familiar fragrance, wildflowers. Then he pulled down the other strap, causing the gown to drop to her waist.

He bent his head and placed kisses on her breasts as he cupped them in his hands. Jenny made a whimpering sound as her hands gripped his head, coaxing him to do more. His tongue darted out and circled one nipple, her breath caught as he teased the rosy peak into pebble hardness.

"Please, Luke," she begged. "I can't stand it."

He drew back and gazed into her eyes. "Good, I don't think I can be patient much longer."

"I don't want to wait, either, Luke. Make love to me." She leaned forward and touched her lips to his. "Show me how to make you happy."

"If you make me any happier, I won't be able to stand it."

"I mean, I want to please you . . . as your wife," she said
shyly.

It took a moment before it dawned on him what she
meant. "You mean, there's never been . . ." He couldn't
speak with the emotion clogging his throat.

She looked up, her gorgeous dark eyes searching his face.
"Does it matter?"

He cupped the back of her neck. "I'll treasure this gift as
I treasure you." He pulled her into his arms and whispered,
"Oh, Jenny, you will please me, never doubt that." He
kissed her once, feeling the hunger building in her as she returned his kisses with equal fervor.

Jenny didn't protest when he slipped the gown from
around her waist and let it drop to the floor. He took a moment to revel in her perfect body, then gently eased her onto
the mattress. He lay beside her and his hands slid across her
silken body, continuing to drive her toward the edge.

"Luke, please," she cried. "I need you." She arched
against him.

"I'm all yours." The truth was, he felt as if he were about
to explode. But this was Jenny's first time, and his only
concern was her pleasure. "I want you ready." His attention quickly went back to his wife lying naked on the bed.

"Oh, Jenny . . . you are beautiful," he whispered as his
gaze traveled up her shapely legs, flat stomach and proud
breasts, until finally his eyes locked with hers. He stood and
slowly tugged off his pajamas, letting them slide to the floor.
It nearly drove him crazy as she examined him boldly, then
raised her eyes to meet his gaze.

"You're beautiful, too," she whispered huskily and held
out her arms. "Make love to me, Luke."

He knelt on the bed and leaned forward. Then his hand
moved across her stomach and lower, slipping his fingers
into the dark hair above her thighs. Jenny gasped and
opened her legs wider for his caress.

Luke took her hand and placed it on his chest, encouraging her to explore on her own, not realizing her sweet touch would be such agony. He stopped her.

"Maybe the next time, honey," he promised as he raised himself over her. He positioned himself between her legs and with more loving words he pushed inside. He felt her resistance give way, cursing himself for having to hurt her. The sweat beaded on his face as Jenny's need kept his rhythm slow, driving the intensity to an unbelievable level.

She matched his strokes with her own urgency until she cried out. He was right there with her, feeling his own explosive release and whispering her name. He hugged her close, her legs holding him prisoner. It took a few minutes to get his emotions under control and he raised away from her, seeing her tears.

"You okay?" He caressed her wet cheeks.

She nodded.

"I'm sorry if I hurt you, Jenny. There just wasn't—"

Jenny placed her finger against his mouth. "It was wonderful." She smiled. "I always wondered why I waited, now I know. It was so special."

Grinning, Luke rolled over and pulled her close to his side. He placed a kiss on her head. "You've had me tied up in knots since the minute I met you. But I'm glad we waited, too."

Jenny looked at her husband. A man didn't make love the way he just had if he didn't care deeply. There were so many questions she wanted to ask her husband. But for now, it was enough that he wanted her.

"I'm glad, too. Otherwise, I might not have gotten you to the altar." She planted kisses on his chest, then worked her way up to his mouth. Her breasts brushed against his skin and she felt his body coming to life again.

"I doubt it. Once with you would never be enough."

Jenny moved against him seductively. "I was hoping you'd say that."

He flipped her onto her back and he was on top. "You're insatiable, woman."

"Are you up to it?" she challenged.

"What do you think?" Luke asked as he slipped inside her and she gasped.

Chapter Twelve

Jenny sat close to Luke as he pulled the Bronco into the driveway leading to the ranch. They were nearly home, but her thoughts were still back at the cabin where they'd spent the last five days in heaven. She blushed, remembering how familiar they'd become with each other... with their bodies. They'd made love often, and whenever they wanted. Some days, they barely made it into clothes. They'd just lit the fireplace that kept the cabin warm and cozy.

Other days, they'd gone on long walks, and had long talks about their hopes and dreams for the future. She'd never felt so close to another human being in her life. She loved Luke Reilly beyond reason. And after the intimacy they'd shared the past week, he had to care about her, too.

Oh, yeah, this marriage was going to work.

"Looks like we have a welcoming committee," Luke said.

Jenny turned toward the porch to see Crissy and Garrett waving at them. As much as she wanted to be alone with Luke, she had missed the children. "I'm glad we stopped and brought them a few presents."

Luke gave her a sideways glance. "You're going to spoil them."

"You're right. I'm planning on spoiling them with lots of love."

"Hey, how about me?"

"I don't think you've been neglected the past few days."

"No, but two kids can sure put a cramp in your spontaneity."

When the car stopped, Jenny opened the door and got out just as Garrett rushed to her and jumped into her arms. "We missed you," he cried.

"Oh, sweetheart, we missed you, too," Jenny said, hugging her new stepson.

Garrett stepped back and looked up at her. "Why couldn't we go?"

Crissy came around the truck with her father. "I already told you, Garrett, kids don't go on honeymoons. They're just for the bride and groom."

"Well, I'm gonna take my kids on my honeymoon."

Crissy rolled her eyes. "Boy, you are so stup—"

"Crissy..." A warning from Luke stopped her words. "He doesn't understand...yet." He laid an arm across his daughter's shoulders.

"I do so," Garrett said stubbornly. "I know that you and Jenny wanted to be alone so you could kiss and hug and all that dumb stuff."

"And we wanted to get to know each other," Jenny tried to explain, feeling her cheeks redden.

Luke bent toward her and gave her a quick kiss on the lips. "Boy, did we ever," he murmured, then with a sexy wink reached inside the truck for their suitcases.

Jenny saw Crissy's curious look and realized the twelve-year-old had a lot of changes to get used to. They wouldn't be so easy for Crissy as for her younger brother. Jenny grabbed her overnight bag and decided that she and her new stepdaughter were going to set aside some time to spend together.

They started for the house. "We brought you both something."

Garrett jumped up and down. "Oh, boy!"

Luke set the bags on the porch. "Kids, take these into the house and we'll be in in a minute."

The five-year-old looked confused. "Why?"

Crissy jumped in. "Because, silly, they want to be alone." Then the children managed to heft the duffel bags and headed up the porch steps.

Jenny looked at her husband. "You didn't have to do that. I don't want Crissy or Garrett to think I'm taking you away from them."

Luke pulled her into his arms. "Look, Jenny, the minute we step into that house, nothing will be simple again. I have to share you with two kids who, I might add, adore you, but will spend all their waking hours trying to take a lot of your time. We may never have a minute of privacy ever again." He dropped a sweet kiss on her lips. "I just wanted to tell you how much these last few days meant to me. You're a special lady, Jenny."

Jenny's heart swelled with his tender words. "You're pretty special to me, too," she whispered and he covered her mouth in a long, heated kiss.

Somewhere in the background, she heard Garrett's whispered voice ask, "What are they doing? Are they kissing?"

Sighing, Luke rested his forehead against hers. "Welcome home, Mrs. Reilly." He swung her up in his arms and she giggled.

Luke managed to open the door and carry her over the threshold and into the living room where the kids and Shelly Hart were standing under a homemade banner. It read, Welcome Home, Mom and Dad.

Jenny's throat suddenly closed with emotion as she and Luke exchanged a quick glance.

"Do you like it?" Garrett asked. "We worked on it all week. Ms. Hart got us the big paper, and I colored all the letters and even stayed in the lines."

"You did a great job, both of you." Jenny noticed Crissy was watching her closely. She went and hugged the girl. "It was so sweet of you."

Crissy smiled. "We had a lot of fun."

"I bet it took a long time." Jenny couldn't take her eyes off the word *Mom.*

"I hope you both were good for Ms. Hart," Luke said. "Did you do your chores?"

Shelly finally joined in and welcomed Jenny home with a hug. "These two were wonderful. They did the dishes, cleaned their rooms and even helped with laundry. Crissy and Garrett were perfect."

Luke frowned at his children, then bent down and took a closer look. "Hold on to those gifts, Jenny, I think we're at the wrong house. I don't know any perfect kids, do you?"

They all giggled. "Oh, Dad, stop teasing." Garrett turned to Jenny. "Can we have our presents now?"

Jenny nodded. "They're in the blue bag." They both attacked the suitcase as she spoke to Shelly. "I hope you'll stay for supper."

The teacher shook her head. "Thank you, but I think tonight is just for family."

Jenny had to agree and she looked at Luke. He, too, seemed relieved that they weren't having guests tonight. He carried Shelly's suitcase to the car.

Jenny and her friend lingered a few minutes on the porch. "You look so happy, Jen."

"I am." She smiled. "I never thought I could ever feel this way." Just then Luke turned around and their eyes met. Her heart began to race as a knowing smile lifted the corners of his sexy mouth.

"It looks like he's pretty taken with you, too," the teacher commented, then sighed. "And he doesn't need me around, either." Shelly hugged Jenny once again and promised to meet for lunch next week.

Luke put his arm around his wife as he watched the compact drive off. "I wish that was us heading back to the cabin." He kissed her. "I'm not ready to share you yet." As if on cue, Crissy's and Garrett's voices drifted outside.

It was music to Jenny's ears. "Looks like you're gonna have to. I guess I better go fix dinner."

Luke wiggled his eyebrows. "And early bedtime for everybody." Together they walked into the house.

In the kitchen, she found a pot of chili, left by Shelly, simmering on the stove. Garrett helped set the table and Crissy served up the food. When the dishes were finished they all played Monopoly until nine.

After the kids' baths, both Jenny and Luke put them down for the night with the promise that tomorrow they could all go into town, and help move the rest of Jenny's things to the ranch. There wasn't another argument after that.

Outside Crissy's room, Luke drew her into his arms and in between kisses, whispered his plans for tonight. Jenny was blushing by the time he shoved her toward the bedroom and told her she had ten minutes.

When she came out of the bathroom twenty minutes later, she found her bare-chested husband already in bed, leaning against the big carved-wood headboard.

Jenny took off her robe, exposing another one of the slinky gowns her sisters-in-law had given her. Seeing the look in Luke's eyes, she would have to be sure to thank them again. "I was kind of hoping that you'd share my shower...."

The next couple of weeks, life was almost perfect. Jenny decided she had married the sexiest man, most tender lover and the sweetest husband in the world. During the day, Luke would call her at work and tell her he'd been thinking about her. The nights, he'd prove to her how much. And the kids. Crissy and Garrett were crazy about having a two-parent family. The only problem there seemed to be Jenny's job, but she explained that in a few weeks, Garrett would be in kindergarten and she wanted to continue working part-time. Luke hadn't been totally convinced, but let her make the choice.

At work, Drew still needled her about the survey, wanting her to talk it up to Luke. Jenny refused. She did offer to have her brother-in-law out to dinner so the men could discuss the situation. She also got hold of Brett when he was in Gillette, and asked him to come and help the meeting along.

Wednesday night, Jenny cooked up her fried chicken and brought home one of Molly's peach pies for dessert, but nothing helped alleviate the solemn mood of the two Reilly brothers seated at the dinner table. After the meal, she ushered the kids up to their rooms and explained that their dad and Uncle Drew needed to talk business.

Before she returned downstairs, the shouting had already started. Jenny hurried into the dining room and found Brett physically trying to keep the brothers apart.

"Luke!" Jenny called as she hurried to the table. "I was hoping you two could talk this out. Not fight. Please, sit down."

Drew sank into his chair. "Jenny's right. We don't need to fight. This is all family here." He looked at Luke. "I was hoping to settle this before we go to court."

"Hell, I didn't start any of this."

"Please, Luke," Jenny said pleadingly. "Just listen."

His eyes narrowed, then finally he nodded.

"Some preliminary studies have been done," Drew began. "The experts agree that there are large mineral deposits on the Double R, and—"

"I don't doubt that," Luke interrupted. "But, I'm not going to sacrifice the beauty of my land to make some fast money in strip mining."

"Can I speak here?" Brett asked. "Now, I've done some checking on the Powder River Basin. I've studied the maps and rock formations on your property. And there are several directions you can go, Luke, that don't involve strip mining."

"Who gave you permission to do testing on my land?" Luke demanded.

Brett glanced at Jenny.

"I asked him to," she admitted, seeing the anger and hurt on her husband's face.

"You had no right."

Drew stood. "Jenny had every right. She's your wife."

Luke kicked his chair away as he got up. He clenched his hands into fists, not wanting anyone to see them trembling. "Why, Jenny? Is it the money?"

"No, Luke," she said. "I didn't want you to end up losing the ranch."

He nodded at Drew. "If he gets his way, there will be no ranch. Or is that what you really want? Being married to a rancher isn't enough?"

Brett jumped to his feet. "Okay, I think we've all said enough. My sister was trying to help."

"Everyone keeps saying that," Luke began, "but I don't remember anyone's being here to help me feed the herd during last winter's blizzard, or at roundup when I'd been branding for twelve hours straight. I especially don't recall my brother helping out when there wasn't enough money for taxes."

Luke got a little satisfaction seeing Drew avert his eyes, but it didn't help the betrayal he felt with Jenny. "But now all of a sudden, everybody here wants to take me to court and destroy everything I've worked for." He had to draw a breath. "Well, I don't need any of you." He marched across the room and grabbed his hat off the hook. "Just everyone leave me alone." He jerked open the door and walked out.

* * *

Jenny sat in the bedroom waiting for Luke. It was after midnight and he still hadn't returned. She knew she had handled things all wrong, but in her heart, she was only trying to help. Her big problem now was how to make things right again.

The door opened and Luke walked in. She drew a breath and stood up. Her eyes combed the tired-looking man she loved. She wanted to go to him and hold him in her arms.

"Luke, I'm sorry. I didn't mean for things to turn out this way."

He pinned her with an angry stare. "How did you mean for them to turn out, Jenny? You truly expected to seduce me out of my land?"

The cutting words pierced her heart. "I never wanted your land. I wanted you."

He made a snorting sound. "I'm supposed to believe that you married me . . . a broke rancher because you love me?"

"I do love you, Luke." But she could see that he wasn't listening. "I don't care about how much money you have. I just didn't want you to lose the ranch."

"Yeah, I remember when Cindy wanted me to sell the mineral rights. She said she loved me, too."

"I'm not Cindy."

"Yeah, you're not. At least she was honest about what she wanted."

Jenny felt the tears building behind her eyes, but her own anger wouldn't allow her to back down. She straightened her shoulders. "I'm sorry you feel that way. I'll never intrude in your business again."

"You're damn right." He went to the closet and pulled out a clean shirt and a pair of jeans.

"Where are you going?"

"I'll be sleeping in the guest room," he said and pulled underwear out of the dresser drawer.

Jenny was suddenly breathless with rage. "Don't think you can treat me like this, Luke Reilly, then decide when you're ready to move back in here."

He paused at the door, then turned around and said, "I think we both need time to cool off."

A week later, Luke was working in the tack room when Brett walked into the barn. "Reilly, we need to talk," he shouted.

Luke came over to the doorway. "I don't think our talking will solve anything."

"It might keep me from beating you senseless," Brett announced.

Luke saw his brother-in-law's clenched fists, but he didn't really care. The mood he'd been in lately, a good fight might make him feel again. "I don't have much time. I'm packing for a hunting trip." He walked back into the tack room and Brett followed him.

"I don't need much time to say what I came to say." Brett drew a long breath and released it. "I want permission to do a survey on the ranch."

Luke gave him an incredulous look. "You're kidding?"

"No, I'm serious. It'll take three days and I can have the results back in four, maybe five."

"Forget it."

"You know the court and your brother aren't going to allow that. Since I've already done some preliminary work, why not just let me finish the job?"

"Yeah, you and your sister went behind my back—"

Before Luke could finish, Brett had him pushed up against the wall. "Listen, Reilly. My sister is already miserable because of you. She's done nothing but try to help you, and if it weren't for your damnable pride you might realize that." Then, as if Brett suddenly realized what he was doing, he released Luke. "So, you gonna let me do the survey or not?"

Luke glared at him. "Do what you damn well please."

Brett glared right back. "Good. That's the smartest thing you've said in a while." He pulled a paper from his back pocket and slapped it down on the counter. "You need to sign it so everything is legal." Brett walked away and Luke started reading the contract.

Brett picked up one of the hunting rifles. "Nice Winchester." He drew it against his shoulder and checked the sight. "You know, when I first met my wife, Jessie, she was aiming a twenty-two at me."

Luke gave his brother-in-law a sideways glance. "Maybe you should have taken the hint," he said as he scribbled his name across the paper.

Brett smiled fondly. "Maybe, but my life wouldn't have been quite as interesting." He put down the rifle, strolled back to Luke and picked up the contract. "Think about how different your life was before Jenny came storming into it."

Luke's Bronco was loaded with equipment, and the horse trailer was hooked up to the back. In a few minutes, when the three hunters arrived, they were heading out for the foothills.

He glanced toward the house. He was aching to go inside and take Jenny in his arms and kiss her until he didn't remember why they'd ever fought. But, dammit, he did remember and it hurt.

Along with the kids, Jenny stepped out onto the porch and his heart began pounding in his chest. She was wearing faded jeans, the bottoms frayed around a pair of buckskin boots. Her red plaid blouse was tucked in, accenting her small waist. She had her hair pulled back into a ponytail and she looked about sixteen, which made his thoughts illegal.

The hard part was he had to say goodbye. He started toward the house and Garrett raced to him.

"How long are you gonna be gone, Dad?"

"For a few days, son. You be good." He hugged the boy, then looked at Crissy. She asked if she could spend Friday night with her friend from school. He agreed if she finished her chores. Then both children disappeared, leaving Jenny and him alone.

This was probably the first time in a week that they'd faced each other since the fight. Yet, as much as he wanted to change things, and although his body ached for his wife, he couldn't forgive what had happened between them.

He reached the porch and looked up to see the pain in Jenny's eyes. It nearly brought him to his knees.

"How long will you be gone?" she asked in a husky voice.

He shrugged. "I'm not sure. No more than three days. Hank's going to handle the herd and feed the stock. If you need anything, Tom will know where to find me."

"Like I've needed you this past week?" She spat out the words contemptuously. "Where have you been, Luke? It's not just me, but the children have noticed, too. They've noticed that you don't touch me anymore... or even come near me. Even Garrett knows we don't share the same bed."

Luke glanced away, suddenly ashamed.

"You better do some hard thinking while you're gone, Luke, because I am." She swiped angrily at the tears on her cheeks. "I will not continue to live this way." With that, she turned, jerked open the screen door and marched into the house.

He wanted to go after her, but just then a truck pulled into the driveway and honked. Damn. He didn't have time to talk now. It would have to wait until he got back. He looked at the door, then went to greet the hunters.

Jenny ran upstairs to the bedroom, crying. She never cried, or at least, before this past week, she never used to. She had hoped that before Luke left on this trip, they could work things out. Had what she'd done been so terrible? She had only been trying to help. She heard the Bronco start up and her back straightened.

She meant every word she'd said to him. She wanted her husband back.

Saturday morning, Jenny sat at the kitchen table, trying to finish her coffee. The half cup sat cooling as she twisted her six-week-old wedding band around her finger. She smiled sadly, remembering the times they'd shared, loving...

Garrett walked into the kitchen still wearing his pajamas. He rubbed the sleep from his eyes and looked at her. "Do we make you sad?"

"Oh, no, sweetie." Jenny got up and went to the boy. "You make me very happy."

"Why don't you smile anymore? You cry...a lot."

"That's not because of you or Crissy. It's because your dad and I are having a few problems."

Tears appeared in the child's eyes. "Crissy said you're getting a divorce and are going away like our other mother did. And we'll never see you again."

"Oh, no, Garrett." Jenny wasn't about to let Luke walk away from their marriage. "There are problems with the ranch. Your dad and Uncle Drew are working things out," she explained as she looked up and discovered Drew and Brett standing at the back door.

Jenny stood as Garrett marched up to confront his uncle. "Why do you have to cause so much trouble? You made everybody sad."

Drew darted a glance at Jenny, but she offered him no sympathy.

"I didn't mean to cause trouble, Garrett," Drew told him.

Jenny got into it then. "But you didn't stop and think about the lives you affected."

Drew swallowed hard. "I guess I didn't." He looked down at his nephew. "But maybe I can straighten things out. Where's Luke?"

"He's guiding a hunting trip."

"Where?"

Jenny shrugged. "Tom's the only one who knows."

He started out the door, but Jenny stopped him. "Don't go after him to start any more trouble, Drew. Because I will personally take you apart."

"She'll do it, too," Brett said.

"I want my family back," Jenny said. "And it looks like you're the only one who can make that happen."

Drew smiled. "I'll do my best."

Luke sat in front of the campfire as the late-September sun was setting. They'd been gone two days, tracking down the elk herd that roamed the foothills on the west section of the ranch. Finally, yesterday morning they'd hit pay dirt, and all three of the hunters he'd brought up had filled their tags. Joe's kill was even a royal seven point bull. It took them the rest of the day to quarter the animals and bring them down on horseback to camp. But they had three good racks to show for their efforts.

Luke stood and walked restlessly around the clearing. Yeah, it had been a successful trip. Or had it?

He used to love to hunt, sleep under the stars. He liked spending time alone just to think and clear his head. Not this time, though. All that he had on his mind the past two days had been Jenny.

After Cindy, he had distanced himself from anything that could hurt him and his children again. For years, he had worked on protecting himself from the pain, but with Jenny he'd gone ahead and fallen in love, anyway. Now he was hurting again.

Suddenly, he spotted someone coming up the rise. Luke went to the edge of the clearing and discovered Drew riding one of his stock horses. What the hell ... Had something happened to the kids? To Jenny?

Luke ran up to his brother and grabbed the reins. "Drew, what's wrong?"

"There are a lot of things wrong." Drew climbed down from his mount. "And we need to talk about them."

Luke glanced at the curious group sitting around the campfire. "This is my brother, Drew. Drew, meet Joe, Matt and Harry."

They all shook hands, and then Luke and Drew walked off to be alone. "Listen, I don't appreciate your coming up here—"

"I don't care," Drew interrupted. "I've been trying to talk to you for over a year. It's a pretty sad state we're in if I have to resort to taking you to court to get you to listen to what I have to say."

"I know what you want."

"No, you don't, Luke," he argued. "You never did. All you think is that everybody is out to take away your damned ranch. Did you ever stop and think about what I wanted?"

"You made it perfectly clear that you never wanted anything to do with ranching."

"How was I supposed to feel? You never asked me to come out and be your partner. I know I went off to school, but you never made me feel like I was a part of the Double R."

"That's because you were happier in town."

"Who said I was happier? When Mom died, I wasn't given a choice. Dad took me in to live with Aunt June and Uncle Charlie. How do you think I felt? I was nine years old, and my mother had just died. At least you had Dad and your home."

Luke had never realized that his brother was so unhappy "But you never said anything."

Drew jerked around. "I never saw you except at Christmas. Then you treated me like a distant cousin. I know I had all the material things a kid could want, but all I really wanted was my dad and...my big brother." Drew's eyes avoided making contact with Luke's. "But it felt like you didn't want me."

"That's not true, Drew. Dad said you'd be better off living in town. I wanted to go in and visit you, but running the ranch kept us busy. Maybe I should have tried when I was older." They made eye contact. "I thought it was the way you wanted it."

"It doesn't matter anymore, Luke. It was a long time ago." He took a breath. "I came to tell you that I'm not taking you to court. You can have the ranch. It belongs to you, anyway." He started to walk away and Luke stopped him.

"Hold it, Drew. Why the sudden change of mind?"

He shrugged. "Let's just say I realized some things aren't worth fighting over. I'm destroying too many people in the process. And I can't stand to cause any more problems between you and Jenny."

"Jenny has nothing to do with this."

"She does, Luke. She's the one hurting, and all she tried to do was help solve our problems. She wants to keep the family together," he said, sitting down on a nearby rock.

"She deceived me."

"No, I did," he admitted. "I'm not proud of it. But I used Jenny to get to you. She only called in her brother to keep you out of court, and hopefully from losing the Double R. She knew how much it meant to you."

It took Luke a while to get his emotions under control. All the time, he kept remembering the cruel things he'd said to his wife.

"How did the survey come out?"

"It's not important."

Luke sat down next to his brother. "It is important. Tell me. What did Murdock come up with?"

Drew's eyes gave away his excitement. "You're not going to believe this, brother, but Brett decided to survey the northern section. You know, the rough terrain that Dad used to say a mountain goat couldn't graze."

Luke knew the area well. It was a wasteland. "Yeah, I remember Dad tried to sell it off years ago, but no one wanted it."

Drew grinned. "Well, it seems that's where Brett feels there are large oil and gas deposits. He said if he were leasing the rights, he'd drill that section."

"What does Jenny think?" Luke was surprised at his own question.

"Maybe you should ask her."

Luke stood, walked a few feet away and leaned against a tree. "She probably wouldn't talk to me."

"The woman loves you. All she ever wanted in return was your love, Luke. She doesn't want to change you, or make you give up the ranch, she's even opened her heart to your kids." Drew shook his head in disbelief. "Do you have any idea what a lucky guy you are?"

Luke's throat tightened. "Yeah. But as usual I'm a little slow in discovering these things."

"I think she'd take you back if you tell her how you feel."

Luke shook his head. "I said too many things...she couldn't forgive."

"Then why did she tell me to come up here and bring you back?"

His heart raced with new hope. "She wants me home?"

"Looks like you have about thirty minutes of daylight and there's going to be a moon tonight. Bet that old horse can find a few shortcuts home."

"But I can't leave. We've got fresh meat to get back."

"I got Tom and Brett to agree to come up in the morning. And I'm staying tonight."

"I don't know what to say."

"Just go after Jenny." Drew went and untied his horse's reins and held them out to his brother. "I don't know how many second chances she's going to give you."

Luke climbed up on the animal. "I hope just one more."

Chapter Thirteen

Luke made it home in record time. After making sure his horse was taken care of, he put him in the stall for the night with extra oats. It was well after nine o'clock when he walked into the dark kitchen, and hung his hat on the wooden peg next to the back door. He walked through the other downstairs rooms to find them deserted, too. He tried to remain calm as he hurried upstairs, then relaxed a little when he found Garrett and Crissy sound asleep in their beds.

After a quick shower and shave in the kids' bathroom to get rid of the traces of a two-day hunt, he pulled on a pair of sweats and headed down the hall. He saw a sliver of light coming from under his bedroom door and knew Jenny was there. He could hear her moving around. He paused at the door and drew a breath, trying to think of something to say that would make her take him back. After releasing a long sigh, he turned the knob and pushed the door open, then froze when he found Jenny pulling her clothes out of the closet and tossing them on the bed.

Was she leaving him?

Jenny looked up and gasped. "Luke! You're home!"

He just stood there and stared at the pile of clothes on the bed. Drew had been wrong, he had run out of time. "By the looks of things, I'm too late."

Jenny combed a shaky hand through her hair. She had to look a mess after cleaning all day. She tried to tuck wayward strands back into her braid. "I didn't expect you home before tomorrow."

"I take it you were planning to be gone before then?"

She searched his dark unreadable eyes. "What are you talking about?"

"Maybe I should just leave and let you finish packing." He walked into the room and shut the door. "But I'm not going to make it that easy for you."

"Packing?" Confused, Jenny looked down at the clothes strewn over the bed. Oh, my God. He thought she was leaving him. She darted a look at Luke. He stood across the room, tall and angry, his legs braced apart, arms folded across his chest.

"I don't run out on people I care about, Luke." Her insides knotted as she came around the bed. "I've wanted to talk out our problems for the past week. You were the one who refused."

He didn't say anything. His face was etched with fatigue and she wanted to run into his arms, but there were too many things unresolved between them.

"I take it Drew found you."

He nodded. "He's staying in camp tonight and bringing everyone back tomorrow."

She continued walking toward him. "So, the two of you came to some sort of understanding?"

"The hell with that. Are you leaving me?"

Jenny tensed. "Is there any reason I should stay?"

"There are two good ones right down the hall," he said. "But is there a good reason between you and me?"

"I think so."

"You didn't trust me enough to tell me about the court hearing. Why wouldn't you let me help?" Jenny felt tears threaten, but she couldn't let them fall.

"It was my problem," he argued. "I was so used to doing things myself that—"

"You didn't trust me."

Luke looked away, ashamed. "I know now I should have. You're my wife and I . . ." His voice trailed off.

Jenny's heart stopped, then began drumming in her chest. "What, Luke . . . ?"

He came closer, his pupils dark and dilated with an intensity she'd never seen before. He reached out and cupped her face in his hands. "I don't want you to leave. I need you in my life." She heard the raw emotion seep into his voice. "Please stay, Jenny."

"Oh, Luke . . ." The last of her words were smothered as he pulled her against him and covered her mouth with his.

The kiss was hungry and desperate. Jenny's arms went around his neck as she eagerly opened to his demanding tongue. She shuddered as he pushed inside, seeking and stroking. Luke's hands were everywhere, roaming across her back, lower to cup her bottom, then pushing against her so she could feel his desire.

She was lost in their special heaven, quickly succumbing to the pleasure. Then Luke's mouth left hers and slowly moved over her face and neck, leaving a trail of hot, wet kisses.

Jenny groaned and tore her mouth away. "No!" She staggered backward as she tried to catch her breath. "This isn't going to work."

Luke looked as dazed as she did. "We seemed to be doing pretty good," he argued.

She fought back a blush. "The bedroom wasn't the source of our problems."

He tossed her a sexy grin and moved toward her. "Too bad we couldn't stay there all the time."

She raised her hand to stop him. "Well, if there's ever going to be a future for us, we have to settle it talking."

He took a deep breath and released it. "Yeah, Drew said the same thing. I guess I've never been much good at sharing."

"Yes, you are. When we were at the cabin, we spent hours talking." They'd also spent hours making love.

Luke turned away. "That was different."

"Why?"

He shrugged. "You're easy to talk to. Besides, they were just hopes and dreams we discussed."

"But I wanted to share your problems. I know how much you love the Double R. I love it, too. Don't you think I want the same thing? I married a rancher, and I expect to be a rancher's wife."

Luke studied her for a moment. "I guess all I remembered was how much Cindy hated it. And since your family is in the oil business, I thought—"

"That I would naturally side with Drew and get you to sell the mineral rights?" she finished for him. Jenny couldn't deny she was hurt. She glanced at the clothes on the bed. "Maybe I don't belong here."

"No!" He reached for her. "Jenny, I was wrong. About so many things, especially in trying to deny my feelings for you. I came back to ask you to forgive me—to beg if I have to."

Luke's hands were trembling. God, he couldn't lose her now. "I promise things will be different. I know now that along with love comes trust. And Jenny..."

"What?" Her wide-eyed gaze searched his face. "What did you say?"

He pulled her into his arms, feeling her sweet breath against his face. "I love you, Jenny Reilly. Please don't leave me."

She froze, then she blinked. "What did you say?" she repeated.

"I said, please don't leave—"

"No! Say the words I've been waiting to hear for a lifetime."

Luke's pulse was racing. "I love you, Jenny."

"Oh, Luke, I love you, too."

"Then why are you leaving?"

She shook her head. "I was just clearing out the room so it could be painted. I love you too much to walk out on our marriage without giving it a chance."

Luke picked her up in his arms. "Thank God. I was so afraid I'd lost you."

"I'm no quitter, Luke Reilly." She finally smiled. "Besides, we have too many dreams to fulfill. I want to see you get your riding-stable business going. Maybe later we could think about building a few cabins to rent out. You know, Lost Pony Cove is a very romantic hideaway when you're with the right person."

Luke's slow grin melted her insides. "Still the matchmaker."

"No, I'm retiring. Shelly and I have been talking about opening up a day-care center. With all the new businesses coming to Last Hope, a lot of parents will need a place to take their children." Her voice softened to a whisper. "Besides, we might need to use the service."

She saw the dumbstruck look on her husband's face and knew what he was thinking. "You're—"

Jenny quickly shook her head. "No. But someday I'd love nothing more than to have our baby."

He swallowed hard and placed his hand on her stomach. "I want that, too." His lips caressed hers so sweetly, it took her breath away.

"First, you should work things out with Drew. And if you decide to drill, I think you should know that I'm a major stockholder in Murdock Oil. But I want don't want that to influence you.''

He kissed her again. "It won't.''

"How about the fact that when my father died, he left me a sizable trust fund?'' She named the amount.

He let loose a soft whistle. "That's some nice pocket change.'' Then he looked embarrassed. "I guess it was crazy of me to think you were after the ranch.''

Jenny was relieved. "I was after you and...Crissy and Garrett. I want to adopt them.'' When he didn't say anything, she raced on. "They need to feel secure about us, about me being a permanent part of their lives.''

His large hand took her face and held it gently. "What did we ever do to deserve you?''

She pulled him down onto the crowded bed. "Not much lately, but maybe you can remedy that. I love you, Luke.''

He shoved the pile of clothes to the floor, then began removing his wife's clothing. "I love you, too, Jenny.'' He laid her down on the mattress. "And I promise, I'm never going to give you any cause to want to leave again.''

She worked on removing his sweatshirt. "Just keep loving me and you'll be stuck with me for the next fifty years, at least.''

"It's not nearly long enough.'' He closed his mouth over hers in a slow, drugging kiss that nearly had her whimpering. Then he raised his head. "I want forever.''

"I thank my lucky stars for the day you came into my life. I don't know what brought you to Wyoming, but I'm sure as hell glad I didn't let you go.''

Jenny raised her head and smiled at her husband. "Why, Luke, you accused me of coming to Wyoming to find a husband. It wasn't until I met you that I set my sights on being a bride. Luke Reilly's bride.''

* * * * *

COMING NEXT MONTH

#1150 WELCOME HOME, DADDY!—Kristin Morgan
Fabulous Fathers
The Murdock marriage was over—or was it? Ross Murdock was
determined to win back his wife, Rachel, especially after discovering another baby was on the way!

#1151 AN UNEXPECTED DELIVERY—Laurie Paige
Bundles of Joy
Talk about labor pains! Any-minute-mom-to-be Stacey Gardenas
was on an assignment when her baby decided to be born. And that
meant her handsome boss, Gareth Clelland, had to help deliver the
child.

#1152 AN IMPROMPTU PROPOSAL—Carla Cassidy
The Baker Brood
Colleen Jensen was desperate—and Gideon Graves was the only
one who could help her. But while searching for Colleen's missing
brother, would Gideon find the way to her heart?

**#1153 THE RANCHER AND THE LOST BRIDE—
Carol Grace**
Parker's sweet little girl made Christine feel like part of the fami-
ly—as did the sparks between her and the rugged rancher!
But could forgotten memories keep Christine from being a *true*
family member?

#1154 AND MOMMY MAKES THREE—Lynn Bulock
Long ago, Matt Viviano gave up on love and happy endings. But
the way Larissa Camden lit up his son's face was a dream come true,
and if Matt wasn't careful, he'd find himself in his own storybook
romance.

#1155 FAMILY MINE—Elizabeth Krueger
Marriage? Meredith Blackmoore refused to even *consider* marrying
Stoney Macreay. She could not ignore her daughter's wish for a
father and Stoney's desire for a family, but could she resist *her* own
need for Stoney?

MILLION DOLLAR SWEEPSTAKES
AND EXTRA BONUS PRIZE DRAWING

No purchase necessary. To enter the sweepstakes, follow the directions published and complete and mail your Official Entry Form. If your Official Entry Form is missing, or you wish to obtain an additional one (limit: one Official Entry Form per request, one request per outer mailing envelope) send a separate, stamped, self-addressed #10 envelope (4 1/8" x 9 1/2") via first class mail to: Million Dollar Sweepstakes and Extra Bonus Prize Drawing Entry Form, P.O. Box 1867, Buffalo, NY 14269-1867. Request must be received no later than January 15, 1998. For eligibility into the sweepstakes, entries must be received no later than March 31, 1998. No liability is assumed for printing errors, lost, late, non-delivered or misdirected entries. Odds of winning are determined by the number of eligible entries distributed and received.

Sweepstakes open to residents of the U.S. (except Puerto Rico), Canada and Europe who are 18 years of age or older. All applicable laws and regulations apply. Sweepstakes offer void wherever prohibited by law. Values of all prizes are in U.S. currency. This sweepstakes is presented by Torstar Corp., its subsidiaries and affiliates, in conjunction with book, merchandise and/or product offerings. For a copy of the Official Rules governing this sweepstakes, send a self-addressed, stamped envelope (WA residents need not affix return postage) to: MILLION DOLLAR SWEEP-STAKES AND EXTRA BONUS PRIZE DRAWING Rules, P.O. Box 4470, Blair, NE 68009-4470, USA.

SWP-ME96

What do women really want to know?

Trust the world's largest publisher of women's fiction to tell you.

HARLEQUIN ULTIMATE GUIDES™

I CAN FIX THAT

A Guide For Women
Who Want To Do It Themselves

This is the only guide a self-reliant woman will ever need to deal with those pesky items that break, wear out or just don't work anymore. Chock-full of friendly advice and straightforward, step-by-step solutions to the trials of everyday life in our gadget-oriented world! So, don't just sit there wondering how to fix the VCR—run to your nearest bookstore for your copy now!

Available this May, at your favorite retail outlet.

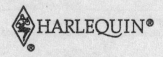

HARLEQUIN®

FIX

SILHOUETTE... Where Passion Lives

Don't miss these Silhouette favorites by some of our most distinguished authors! And now you can receive a discount by ordering two or more titles!

SD#05849	MYSTERY LADY by Jackie Merritt	$2.99	☐
SD#05867	THE BABY DOCTOR	$2.99 U.S.	☐
	by Peggy Moreland	$3.50 CAN.	☐
IM#07610	SURROGATE DAD	$3.50 U.S.	☐
	by Marion Smith Collins	$3.99 CAN.	☐
IM#07616	EYEWITNESS	$3.50 U.S.	☐
	by Kathleen Creighton	$3.99 CAN.	☐
SE#09934	THE ADVENTURER	$3.50 U.S.	☐
	by Diana Whitney	$3.99 CAN.	☐
SE#09916	AN INTERRUPTED MARRIAGE	$3.50 U.S.	☐
	by Laurey Bright	$3.99 CAN.	☐
SR#19050	MISS SCROOGE	$2.75 U.S.	☐
	by Toni Collins	$3.25 CAN.	☐
SR#08994	CALEB'S SON	$2.75	☐
	by Laurie Paige		
YT#52001	WANTED: PERFECT PARTNER	$3.50 U.S.	☐
	by Debbie Macomber	$3.99 CAN.	☐
YT#52002	LISTEN UP, LOVER	$3.50 U.S.	☐
	by Lori Herter	$3.99 CAN.	☐
	(limited quantities available on certain titles)		

TOTAL AMOUNT	$_____
DEDUCT: 10% DISCOUNT FOR 2+ BOOKS	$_____
POSTAGE & HANDLING	$_____
($1.00 for one book, 50¢ for each additional)	
APPLICABLE TAXES**	$_____
TOTAL PAYABLE	$_____
(check or money order—please do not send cash)	

To order, send the completed form with your name, address, zip or postal code, along with a check or money order for the total above, payable to Silhouette Books, to: **In the U.S.:** 3010 Walden Avenue, P.O. Box 9077, Buffalo, NY 14269-9077; **In Canada:** P.O. Box 636, Fort Erie, Ontario, L2A 5X3.

Name:_____

Address:_____ City:_____

State/Prov.:_____ Zip/Postal Code:_____

**New York residents remit applicable sales taxes.
  Canadian residents remit applicable GST and provincial taxes.   SBACK-MM2

Silhouette®

**THIS FABULOUS FATHER IS ABOUT
TO GET A SECOND CHANCE AT MARRIAGE—
AND FATHERHOOD!**

WELCOME HOME, DADDY!
by Kristin Morgan

One night with her soon-to-be ex-husband left Rachel Murdock
confused—and pregnant! Ross was determined to romance her
back into his arms, but only a miracle would convince Rachel
that her handsome husband was a changed man. And that miracle
was only a due date away!

Don't miss **WELCOME HOME, DADDY!**
by Kristin Morgan, available in May, only from

FF596

As seen on TV!
Free Gift Offer

With a Free Gift proof-of-purchase from any Silhouette® book,
you can receive a beautiful cubic zirconia pendant.

This gorgeous marquise-shaped stone is a genuine cubic
zirconia—accented by an 18" gold tone necklace.
(Approximate retail value $19.95)

Send for yours today...
compliments of ▼ *Silhouette*®

To receive your free gift, a cubic zirconia pendant, send us one original proof-of-
purchase, photocopies not accepted, from the back of any Silhouette Romance™,
Silhouette Desire®, Silhouette Special Edition®, Silhouette Intimate Moments®
or Silhouette Shadows™ title available in February, March or April at your favorite
retail outlet, together with the Free Gift Certificate, plus a check or money order for
$1.75 U.S./$2.25 CAN. (do not send cash) to cover postage and handling, payable
to Silhouette Free Gift Offer. We will send you the specified gift. Allow 6 to 8 weeks for
delivery. Offer good until April 30, 1996 or while quantities last. Offer valid in the U.S. and
Canada only.

Free Gift Certificate

Name: _____

Address: _____

City: _____ State/Province: _____ Zip/Postal Code: _____

Mail this certificate, one proof-of-purchase and a check or money order for postage
and handling to: SILHOUETTE FREE GIFT OFFER 1996. In the U.S.: 3010 Walden
Avenue, P.O. Box 9057, Buffalo NY 14269-9057. In Canada: P.O. Box 622, Fort Erie,

---

FREE GIFT OFFER   079-KBZ-R
ONE PROOF-OF-PURCHASE
To collect your fabulous FREE GIFT, a cubic zirconia pendant, you must include this
original proof-of-purchase for each gift with the properly completed Free Gift Certificate.

079-KBZ-R